SWEET DREAMS

MARIKA RAY

SWEET Dreams

ISBN-13:
978-0-9992981-0-7 (E-book Edition)
978-0-9992981-1-4 (Print Edition)

Major thanks to these fabulous ladies:
Proofreader: **Virginia Tesi Carey**
Cover Artist: **Amy Queau, Q Design**

DEDICATION

This first book of mine is dedicated to my ten-year-old daughter, without whom, this book would not exist. She helped me flesh out the basic story line, along with the main characters' names. She never doubted that her mom would be a published author one day, even when my novel was just a story I rambled on about at bedtime while we snuggled.

Sea otters for life, baby!

∾

*I*t was a busy Friday night at Freddie's, a popular Mexican restaurant right on Main Street with a view of the beach, and all the people were enjoying the pier view of the sunset. The music was thumping through the many speakers placed inside the bar and out on the deck. The lights were low, the beer was flowing, and the locals had come out in full force to celebrate the weekend. It was too early in the season for a rush of tourists, so I'd agreed to a night out after weeks of begging from Bailey, my roommate and best friend. If I were to make an appearance at Freddie's it would be before the craziness started. Last year, I made the mistake of coming here on July 3rd and the number of wasted guys was an immediate turn off. The three-way girl-on-girl tussle, complete with hair pulling, was interesting too.

Tonight was definitely more tame and at least tolerable in my book. I was one beer into the evening, getting cozy with the tortilla chip bowl, when my roommate gave me the heads-up. "Esa, the dark-haired guy over there is totally checking you out, girlie," she said with minimal lip movement.

"Ah shit, you know I'm not interested in any of that. Don't look at him," I answered her, shoving another salsa laden chip into my mouth.

Of course, she made eye contact with him anyway, then smiled and tilted her head in my direction. "Oh, would you look at that, he's coming over here," she exclaimed, playfully shocked.

If looks could kill, she would have incinerated on the spot. This was so not what I wanted.

"Hey, can I buy you another beer?" dark-haired guy asked as he wedged in next to me. He wasn't bad looking but the fraternity guy smirk was not helping his case. Nor was the major waft of yeasty beer smell that came from his direction.

"No, thanks, I'm good. In fact, I was going to hit the bathroom and then get out of here. Thanks anyway though," I responded, then grabbed my bag to leave the table. I didn't wait for his reply as I made my way to the bathroom down the hallway in the far corner. I didn't even feel guilty that I left my best friend to deal with him. She brought him over, she could get him to leave, right?

Just as I reached the door to the women's, someone grabbed my elbow and pulled me back. I looked up into frat guy's determined face.

"Ah come on, honey, you don't need to rush off like dat. You can a' least get to know me first, huh?" he slurred out. I wanted to wipe the sly grin off his face with a sharp comeback, but instead I took a deep breath and smoothed out my facial expression. He was intoxicated. Who knew how mean he could get?

"Listen. I'm not interested. Please let go of my arm," I said in my most stern voice.

"Hey, that's not very nice. You don't need to be a bitch."

Did he really think whining and then calling me a bitch would help him get laid? Red flags were flying left and right. This guy was bad news.

Before I could get another word out, a tall, dark-haired guy walked by me, pushing his shoulder into drunk frat boy. The hand gripping my elbow dropped, and I used the opportunity to duck around them both and move back into the more populated bar area where my roommate was rushing up to find me. The two boys were now face to face in one of those weird macho show-downs guys do. Drunk guy eventually backed down and slunk away as he realized the other guy was taller, bigger, and less inebriated.

My rescuer was off-the-charts hot in his lifeguard polo and red shorts, but I focused on his face when he asked if I was okay. I nodded yes. He jerked his chin up in the cool guy equivalent of nodding and walked away.

And that my friends, was my cue to leave. This wasn't my scene. And I sure as shit wasn't looking for a guy. Drunk or gorgeous, it didn't matter. Time to go home.

I grabbed Bailey and hustled her out the door with me.

Rule number one of bestie girl code: you didn't leave a bestie behind.

A friend and a bestie were two different things. Trusting a person with your very life? Someone who totally understood you, saw your crazy and not only didn't pass judgement, but liked your crazy? That right there was a bestie. I knew it was rare to find that connection with anyone, considering it had only happened once in my twenty-six years on this earth, which was why I absolutely adored my best friend Bailey.

We met in high school when life was awkward and feelings were easily bruised. I first saw her when I entered science class the first day of freshman year. She was ripping into some guy sitting next to her who had rolled his eyes at her outfit. The poor guy didn't even know what hit him when she verbally whipped him with her sassy comeback. He vacated the seat for friendlier pastures and I found myself taking his spot. I was drawn to her confidence, to her 'take no shit' attitude. I wanted that for myself.

You see, I was the quiet one. I observed people and situations more than I got involved in them. I wasn't the life of the party; hell, I wasn't even invited to the party. I wasn't an outcast or anything. I just wasn't noticed much, which was usually fine by me, but I wanted to turn things around in high school and live a little. I decided, right there on the spot, someone like Bailey was the perfect person to have by my side.

I could remember our first words like it was yesterday.

"You got something to say about my kickass outfit too?" Bailey asked with a raised eyebrow.

Realizing she was talking to me, I quickly reassured her. "Yeah, I do. I think you look great in it. And I like whatever you said to that jerk-off. Teach me how to do that."

She stared at me for a long moment, then grinned. "All right. Here we go. Let's do this."

And that was that. A budding friendship began, escalating quickly to Besties with a capital B. We were inseparable all four years of high school. Where she was flash and heat, I was cool and calm. When she dropped sass and attitude, I followed up with sunshine and steady determination. We were different in a lot of ways, except for our commitment to each other. We had each others' backs, and we both had plans for our futures. We graduated high school and applied to the same colleges. Where one went, the other would too. And so we found ourselves at University of San Diego sharing a dorm on campus, her major Fashion Design, and mine Business.

Those plans for our future took a serious hit when my parents were killed in a car accident on the I-405 in Long Beach when they were taking a random day trip to the Aquarium. I had a new reason to hate that freeway.

Bailey and I were in our second year of college when it happened. I was in BioChem 2 when the police pulled me from class to deliver the news. I was in total shock when I texted Bailey to leave her English Lit class and find me. The police were still telling me the details of what happened when she burst into the hall and pulled me to her side, her arms holding me upright. I made the officers start over because Bailey needed to hear it too. They had loved her like their own daughter and she ate that love right up. This would crush us both.

I didn't shed one tear till the next day. And then it was like I couldn't stop, my eyes leaking the heartache that seemed a new, permanent part of my life.

Long story short, that was a really rough time. I completely fell apart and Bailey held me together. When I wanted to just drift away in my grief, give up on college, and go back home to Huntington Beach, Bailey wouldn't let me. She said all the right things, did all the right things, and got me in to see the college counselor on a regular basis.

I eventually pulled through and I owe that to Bailey.

She. Was. Solid.

"Okay girl, we gotta slow down," Bailey gasped. We slowed to a fast walk but kept moving toward the pier.

It was Monday afternoon in early spring and both Bailey and I had the day off. We decided there wasn't anything better than a run on the beach, especially since there were a lot more lifeguards on duty now that spring break was in full swing. I may be surrounded by chocolate all day long, but a girl still needs her eye candy, know what I mean? Run to burn calories so I can drink more chocolate and eyeball hot lifeguards while doing it. Double bonus! This was quickly becoming a favorite weekly routine for us.

"Yeah, I know what you mean. I'd much rather be at the gym throwing around some weights. This running shit is hard!" I had curves built from weight training and a few too many hot chocolates. I swear I wasn't built for running, but I knew it was good for me. I may not have an ex-boyfriend grabbing my belly roll anymore but that little voice in my head was still there. I was getting better at punching it in the face and getting it to pipe down, but it still popped up more often than I'd like.

Junior year of college I met a charming classmate, and he seemed totally into me. Day dreams of tall, dark, and handsome took over my days and made my boring classes fly by. He'd meet up with me in-between classes, take me to lunch at the school cafeteria, and help me study at my dorm. He was so attentive, I found myself slowly pulling away from Bailey and my other friends to spend more of my days and nights with him. He made my grieving, reluctant heart want to feel again.

Unfortunately, once I trusted him, he seemed to change overnight. Gone was the sweet, in its place an underhanded monster dressed like my boyfriend. His digs were subtle enough not to ring any warning bells, but enough to damage my self-esteem. When I gathered the courage to call him on his bullshit, he would laugh it off, saying he was joking or I was simply making too much out of it.

All the sass and confidence I emulated under Bailey's tutelage was quietly forgotten as I compromised myself for him. I'd felt adrift since my parents died. Add in my quiet nature, along with my limited dating experience, and that all combined to leave me vulnerable. And he totally capitalized on that for a few long, confusing months.

Bailey finally intervened and made me see the light. I broke up with Rylan, and he ended up dropping out of school when months went by and I refused to speak to him. With him gone, I could focus back on school and building the life I wanted for myself. No more assholes, no more allowing life to happen to me. I was ready to kick some ass and build my dream life.

The anger over his emotional abuse, and the grief over my parents, shifted forms over time, but didn't lessen in intensity. All that emotion was funneled into school, planning for my business, and studiously avoiding men at all costs.

"Let's pick it up to the pier and then walk back?" Bailey asked after we'd caught our breaths and my brain had taken a wrong turn that took me through my past.

"Let's do it."

We picked it back up to a run and made our way to the pier. After we touched the concrete pillar and turned around, we had a mile to get back to Beach Blvd & PCH where we tied up our bikes. Doesn't sound like a very long distance until you're running it in the soft sand, wind blowing hair in your face and having to dart around small children building sand castles.

We'd completed a couple more spurts of jogging when we slowed down for our final cool down walk at lifeguard tower seventeen. I had a decent sweat going on and the burn in my legs was real. It was unusually warm that afternoon, so I veered into the surf to get my feet wet and cool off quicker. I was only a few steps in when I felt a stabbing sensation in my right foot.

"Ouch! Holy shit!" I yelped in a high-pitched voice that would have embarrassed me if the pain in my foot wasn't so damn distracting.

"Esa? What's wrong?" Bailey came running down into the surf after me.

"Wait! Stay back!" I said as I inched out of the water. Once I cleared the water's edge, I sat down and brought my foot closer to my face. "I don't know what that was but my foot feels like it's on fire."

"Let me see," Bailey insisted. She got up close to my foot without touching it and gave it a thorough inspection. "Babe, I think you got stung by a jellyfish!"

"You think? I didn't even see anything! What do I do to make it stop stinging?" I was edging toward full on panic by now. The sting was escalating and I had no clue what to do with a jellyfish injury. Jellyfish sting? Cut? What the hell do you even call it when a jellyfish wraps around your skin and does its thing?

"Okay, first, you gotta calm down. Let me go grab the lifeguard. He'll know what to do." Bailey hopped up and ran toward the tower where I spotted a tall, blond lifeguard. They both came running back to where I remained seated in the sand. He immediately crouched down and took a look at my foot. While his head was down, I caught an up-close eyeful of hottie lifeguard hair, arms, and chest. A nice waft of sunscreen and sunshine hit my nose, and I leaned a little closer to catch another whiff. Suddenly the pain in my foot didn't seem all that bad.

Tan muscle shifted as he lifted my foot, gently tracing a path down my calf with one long finger. The jellyfish sting faded to the background as I felt that caress as a delicious ache in my belly.

"Yep, I think your friend here is right. This looks like a jellyfish sting and we've had reports of them all along the coast the last couple of days," he said, looking up and catching my eyes.

His eyes bore into mine, making me forget who I was and why I was here. They were a turquoise blue with a ring of darker blue around the edge. They looked friendly, like his eyes were smiling at me, regardless of what his mouth was doing. But what really caught my attention was the depth to his eyes that told me he saw me, the real me. Which was straight up crazy as we'd just met, but there it was. He saw me.

2

"*D*o you have any shortness of breath?" the lifeguard asked me in a lowered, more intimate voice, still focused entirely on me.

His words hung in the air as I tried to get my brain to function. "Um, no. I mean, we were just running which usually makes me short of breath, but nothing out of the ordinary." I couldn't stop staring into his eyes.

"Doesn't look like you're having an allergic reaction then, so let's put some vinegar on your foot and see if that stops the stinging. I'll be right back." He gently placed my foot back down on the sand and hopped up to ran back to the lifeguard tower. I instantly missed his presence, even as I twisted around to watch him run.

His upper body had just the right amount of muscle to be fit, but he wasn't too bulky. His run was athletic and you could tell the guy worked out on the regular based on the natural v-taper he had going on from his wide shoulders to his narrow waist. Plus, no guy has a tight butt like that unless he works out.

Apparently, Bailey was ogling him too. "Girl, that man is ridiculous! You better get his name. Maybe his number would be good too. You know, to call and thank him for his fine life-guarding services," Bailey said with a grin. "I think he's into you. Did you see how long he held your leg? And what was with all the touching?"

"Shh, he'll hear you. And quit staring at him," I whisper-yelled back. I was trying to act cool when in reality, I was straight up discombobulated. Only thing I knew was I didn't want Bailey looking at him like that. I quickly erased my frown and twisted back around as he headed back toward me, vinegar in hand. He dropped down to the sand in front of me and put his warm hand back on my leg, putting him in close proximity.

"Okay, let's pour this on here. After you get home, you may want to put some ice on it if it continues to bother you." He dripped the vinegar onto my foot slowly. "No running for a few days while you let this heal."

"Mmmh..." I let out a low groan as the stinging began to recede. He whipped his head up and stared at me, vinegar dripping onto the sand instead of my foot. I felt my cheeks heating up as I realized my unintentional groan may have been a little suggestive. He cleared his throat, broke eye contact, and got the vinegar back on my foot, which I greatly appreciated, but I also regretted the lost eye contact.

"So, you live around here?" He continued to rub my upper calf, which was doing crazy things to my internal organs. The whole lower half of my body was on fire.

"Yeah, I, um, live just north of here off Beach Blvd," I responded, not recognizing the soft, breathy voice that came out of me. I was acting like a damsel in distress and I didn't like it one bit.

"Heck yes, she lives around here! Comes running on the beach with me all the time. I'm surprised we haven't seen you before," Bailey interjected, making me startle. I'd completely forgotten she was here. Oh boy, if I knew Bailey, and I did, this could get embarrassing. She was in full flirt mode for my benefit.

"Well I'm usually the supervisor in the mobile unit, but we're short staffed today, so I took a tower," he answered Bailey while still looking at me. "I'm Ivan, by the way." He broke out into a stunning smile. I blinked.

"Hey Ivan, I'm Bailey and this is my best friend Esa," Bailey jumped in again. "You know, you better get Esa's number since you'll want to check in on her later to make sure her foot's okay, right?"

"Bailey!" I snapped, coming out of my Ivan-fog long enough to realize she was totally crossing the line.

She shrugged like she couldn't help herself, which was probably true.

Ivan let out a soft chuckle, bringing my focus back to him.

"I'm sorry, really. I don't know why I even bring her with me sometimes. She has no filter," I stammered, unable to look him in the eye. "I'm sure my foot will be fine."

"I think you'll be just fine too, but your friend here makes a good point. I want to make sure my first aid skills are still top-notch. Probably gonna need to contact you later to check in." That smile of his was now a sexy smirk.

"What's your number, Ivan? I've got Esa's phone here. I'll just text yours so you'll have her number," Bailey piped in again. I would have to have a word with her later. And confiscate my phone from her fashion fanny pack. She just lost privileges. I wasn't sure at all if I wanted this guy to have my phone number. I was more than a little nervous about what a simple smile from him did to my breathing.

As numbers were exchanged, I decided to end this debacle. My foot felt a million times better, and it was time to make my exit. "I hate to be a party downer but we gotta get back home," I said firmly.

I started to push up to stand, when Ivan crouched down again and said, "Oh, no you don't. Not a good idea to walk on that foot so soon. And what the hell is a party downer?" He had an amused expression on his face. His eyes crinkled at the corners when he smiled, highlighted by his solid tan.

Ah crap, I did it again.

"Don't worry about her. She's always mixing up phrases in highly entertaining ways. It's one of her many charms," Bailey said, helping me out before turning to walk back toward our bikes.

"Let me guess, party pooper mixed with Debbie Downer?" Ivan said before he scooped me up with one arm around my back and the other under my knees. All thoughts of mixed up phrases or protesting the need for help left me as I was pressed up against his body. I felt his firm chest where my hand landed on it. He was radiating heat and my first instinct was to cuddle in close for more. My body betrayed me by full body shivering before I could control it. Our faces were now just inches apart as he smiled down at me. I wrapped my arm around his neck and hung on for dear life. It was not a hardship.

"I'll carry you to your car," he said softly, not moving, as if waiting for my permission.

I nodded my head, still a little unsure how I ended up in his arms. "We rode bikes. Tied up over there." No sooner were the words out then he began to carry me across the sand. "Are you sure you want to carry me all the way over there? It's pretty far and I'm sure I'm a little too heavy for this," I offered up, feeling more than a little embarrassed by the whole thing.

He halted again, letting Bailey get ahead of us. "Are you

saying I'm not strong enough to carry you a few feet?" He quirked a blond eyebrow.

I was pretty sure he was joking with me, but there was also a hard edge to his voice that made me wonder.

"Well no, I'm just saying-"

"That must be what you're saying because there's no way a girl as beautiful as you could possibly think that she's too heavy to be carried," he said in a soft, sweet tone. Then he continued a little louder with a hint of a smile. "So, I'm left to think that you doubt my physical abilities. Is that right?"

I was getting the feeling he didn't like my self-deprecation, and since I didn't either, I dropped my self-consciousness, and decided to engage in some of my own flirting. Girl gotta practice. "Well, I don't know you that well yet. I guess you'll have to show me what you can do." That sounded much better. That was the confident girl I'd worked so hard to become.

I lifted my hand from his chest and moved some of his wavy hair out of his eye since his hands were full. His hair was thick and had some wave to it, making me want to keep running my hand through it.

Ivan had a definite gleam in those turquoise eyes, because of my comment or my touch, I wasn't sure. But those eyes were intense, and they were focused entirely on me. "That's a challenge I think I'll enjoy, Esa."

Then he full out ran with me bouncing around in his strong arms. I held on tight and enjoyed the ride. I hadn't had this much fun being ridiculous and impulsive in years. So much so I threw my head back and laughed at how ridiculous we must look bouncing across the sand.

We made it to the bikes and to my disappointment Ivan put me down so my feet hit the sand, but not before I got to feel his hard body on the slide down. I still had a smile on my face as he kept his hands on my waist, looking intently in my eyes. "I'll call you tonight to check in on you. And I look forward to showing you all I can do and getting to know you more. I also hope to hear more of that gorgeous laugh of yours. Be safe riding home, Esa." He gave my waist a squeeze, turned, and ran back to the lifeguard tower.

I stood there watching him go, too stunned to answer him.

"Hell, I need a cold shower just watching you two. That was some seriously hot flirting there, girl," Bailey said, breaking me out of my mini-coma.

I didn't know if I'd take it that far, but any flirting with a guy, rather than just an outright rejection, was improvement for me. I couldn't help the huge smile taking over my face as I agreed with her and got on my bike. The picture of those eyes smiling at me was forever burned into my brain. I'd never been so happy to have a close encounter with a jellyfish.

It wasn't until later that night I began to wonder what I'd gotten myself into with attempts at flirting. I mean, Bailey and I were laser focused on our careers. I didn't have time for distraction in the form of a hot lifeguard. In fact, just remembering how we got Bailey her dream job made me laugh out loud in my empty bedroom.

When we finally graduated from college, Bailey was looking for a job as a personal shopper at a high-end retailer. As a best friend would, I knew I had to help her attain her dream. So, I cashed out the last of my parents' life insurance money and hatched a brilliant scheme. Don't freak out on me, I used the life insurance money wisely to pay for my college education. I was always responsible with my finances, but I was due a little play time and as a double bonus, I could help Bailey.

We researched the hiring manager at Nordstrom at Fashion Island, cased the place to know when she worked, and then sprang into action. On a Tuesday afternoon, Bailey strutted through the second level of Nordie's looking fabulous in her typical style. She was classically beautiful with her dark smooth skin, tall with legs that went on forever, big, curly hair, and bright smile. She added her own spin on cool with her accessories, creating a look that exuded confidence and an energy that made you want to be around her.

As all eyes tracked her movement through the racks, she grabbed a top, a pair of pants, and a scarf, assembling them into a makeshift outfit right on the rack. I casually walked by, stopped, backtracked, and began the show.

"Oh my God! That looks so beautiful! Do you think that would work on my body type?" I asked with obvious excitement.

Bailey turned to me, flashed a smile, and said, "For sure it would work on you! Let's change the scarf out for a cooler color, but other than that, this outfit looks like it was made for you. Want to try it on?"

"Heck, yeah I do! I'm so glad I ran right into you. Nordstrom is so good with having their personal shoppers out on the floor helping us fashion impaired people," I went on gushing.

"Oh no, honey, I don't work here. I just love fashion and dressing women so they feel confident in their clothes," Bailey said with convincing passion. And it was true. That's why she spent four years getting her degree in fashion.

We took the party to the fitting rooms and two hours later I walked out with five complete outfits, shoes, accessories, and undergarments included. This spending spree did not go unnoticed by the Nordstrom employees. After I sashayed out with my haul, Bailey was approached by our target, the hiring boss, and offered a job on the spot. I wasn't surprised, and I certainly didn't feel bad about our scheme. Those outfits kicked ass and I couldn't wait to wear them as I realized my own dream: owning a business in Surf City, USA.

For as long as I could remember, I've loved hot chocolate. Not like normal little kids like it. It wasn't just the whipped cream, or the chocolaty taste, or the fact that it was a warm, cozy drink. I was flat out obsessed with it. I'd made thousands of cups of hot chocolate, slowly perfecting my recipes. Yes, recipes plural, upwards of fifty. My friends and family got tired of always having to taste my recipes but my mom encouraged me to keep doing it. No basic Starbucks coffee runs for me as a college student. I wanted quality hot chocolate that only I could make at home.

My chocolate obsession took a brief hiatus when I was dating Rylan since he thought I was getting a little too curvy because of all the chocolate. I mean really, I should have seen the red flag for what it was; any man who tries to separate a woman from her chocolate is flat out insane.

I planned to open a shop when I was out of college and my mom would help me run it. She'd do the website and the cash register, I'd handle the menu offerings and choose the shop decor. In a grand departure from the plan, she died before that could happen. But my chocolate dreams didn't.

Since I used the last of my savings to pay off my college education and kick start Bailey's personal shopper dreams, I worked part-time at a local bakery to save up the cash needed to start my shop. It took me almost six months, but I was finally ready. There was a new retail shopping center, Pacific City, being built right on Pacific Coast Highway, or PCH as the locals called it. High end shops were committing to retail space in the new center and I wanted in. This would be the place to shop, eat, and once the condos were built behind it, hang out with a warm cup of gourmet hot chocolate. If determination and heart were enough to keep a company afloat, there was no doubt mine would thrive.

My only hurdle was a middle-aged man on the committee that tried to block me from renting space. He felt that as a young woman untested in the business world, I was not a good fit for Pacific City and should settle for elsewhere. He was quite vocal about his dislike for me and my business idea. I'm not sure what I ever did to piss him off, but damn, that guy had it in for me. I had to work that much harder by going around him and pleading my case to the head honcho of the management company, before I was finally granted a rental space.

The work was worth it as the space was perfect. All white decor with pops of black and dusty pink. My shop name, 'Chocolate Dreams' was proudly posted on the outside awning, on the large front window, and on the old-fashioned chalk menu board behind the long white counter. A glass case sat next to the counter, filled with bakery items to complement the hot chocolate varieties. Lastly, a long window on the back wall gave a picture-perfect view of the ocean. Wherever my eye looked, it found delight. Which was by design. I wanted my customers' senses bombarded, in a good way, when they entered my shop.

We officially opened over the holidays with my peppermint hot chocolate being a best seller. Nothing like a hint of peppermint chocolate, thick homemade whipped cream topped with mint shavings to make your mouth happy when it was cold and rainy outside. Of course, salted caramel hot chocolate, mocha chip hot chocolate, and marshmallow dream hot chocolate were popular choices too. Mouth orgasms were guaranteed, and I was seriously considering making that my official slogan. Sorry mom.

Sales continued to be good through the first of the year. Bailey was loving her job outfitting the high-end population of Newport Beach. The ex-boyfriend and his abuse were history. I lived the beach life in sunny California. Life was comfortable. A little lonely, but steady.

What I still hadn't learned was that you couldn't control what life threw at you. When you least expected it, you could get the best--and sometimes the worst--things in life thrown at you.

My cell phone ringing interrupted my trip down memory lane. Ivan's name lit up my screen, sending my heartbeat into overdrive. I let it ring for a few seconds before answering it. I mean, come on, I wasn't into the dating scene, but even I knew I shouldn't look overly eager. Taking a deep breath to calm my shaking hands, I answered.

"Esa? This is Ivan," he responded. "How's that jellyfish sting feeling this evening?"

Just his deep voice caused a big smile to bloom on my face. My heart was still racing, but something was going on in my stomach now too.

"Well...I had this awesome lifeguard treat it with vinegar today which helped take away the sting, so it's feeling pretty good," I nearly high-fived myself for doing a little more light flirting.

"Sounds like that lifeguard totally knew what he was doing. And I have it on good authority he enjoyed spending time with you today." Ivan's tone that told me that, he too, was smiling into the phone.

"Well, maybe you could be a sweetheart and let him know his athletic abilities more than passed the test." I may have sounded all confident and flirty but the reality was my hands were getting sweaty. Why oh why did I have to get so nervous talking to a gorgeous guy?

"Hmm, I think you better tell him yourself. Maybe tomorrow morning? Over coffee?" Ivan asked. He sounded pretty confident. Too confident. I wasn't sure I was up for this kind of verbal sparring for any length of time. I wasn't sure I was up for any kind of relationship. But there was something about his blue eyes and the way he really looked at me today on the beach that made me want to say yes. Bailey kept telling me that not all guys were like my ex, and I believed her, but actually giving someone else a chance scared the crap out of me. But it was just coffee. I could just do this one little date and use it as a test run for the future. A way to practice interacting with a guy and trying out my new confidence. A girl has to get out there and practice, amiright? Okay, I was doing it.

"Esa? Are you still there?" Ivan's voice came over the line, startling me from my thoughts.

"Oops, sorry about that. Yes, I'd love to meet up with you tomorrow. But only if the place has hot chocolate. I'm not a coffee girl." Better he knew up front that chocolate was my thing. And I wouldn't be taking any crap for it either. Never again.

"Great! I'll meet you at the coffee shop off Beach and Atlanta. I know for a fact they serve hot chocolate. I don't work till mid-morning, so does eight work for you?"

"Yep, I'll see you there!" I responded before I had a chance to overthink it.

The jelly fish sting must have been affecting my brain. I was actually going out on a date.

With a virtual stranger.

3

I was five minutes early to our coffee/hot chocolate non-date the following morning. I liked getting places early and settling in before people arrived. Maybe it's an introvert thing. I liked to sit, get the lay of the land, observe other people, and have time to gear up for the ensuing conversation marathon.

However, that wouldn't happen today as I saw Ivan already sitting at a table watching the front door as I entered. He smiled and stood up as I approached. He was looking damn fine in a fresh, white polo shirt and the trademark lifeguard red board shorts.

"Hey, you're early!" I said, right before he pulled me into his body with a gentle hug. He smelled like the same sunscreen from yesterday, blended nicely with soap this morning. I was getting the sense he liked a lot of bodily contact.

"Good morning! I just think you should never keep a beautiful woman waiting," Ivan responded as he let me out of the hug. He kept one hand on my waist and I didn't know if he even realized he was still touching me. "Did you want whipped cream on that hot chocolate?"

"It's not really hot chocolate if it doesn't have whipped cream," I joked.

"I like the way you think. Why don't you have a seat to save our table and I'll go order for us," Ivan said as he helped me into the chair. He finally lost contact with me as he moved to stand in line. If I was being honest with myself, I already missed his touch. There was something very warm and welcoming about him. His touch wasn't too forward, it was just nice. If I wasn't so busy being nervous, I bet I'd love those hugs and touches.

I may not have been able to touch him right then, but I tracked him across the store with my eyes. I couldn't pass up the perfect opportunity for me to study him in line without being caught staring. He was tall, I'd guess 6'3", with stereotypical California good looks. Blond, shaggy hair that was kept long on top, but short on the sides. Those blue eyes that could mesmerize you with their intensity. His muscular physique really was yummy. Just enough muscle to make you look twice and appreciate it. I was thinking he was late 20's, probably older than me if he was already a supervisor, rather than just a regular lifeguard.

Let's be real: he was straight up gorgeous. And that was just talking about his body. Add in the sweetness and the soul-searching blue eyed gaze and he probably had women falling at his feet. I'd have to ask around and see if he had a reputation. I just had a hard time believing that a man that delectable, and not taken, wasn't also a total player. But, I reminded myself, this was just a trial run, a practice, for testing out my flirting skills. It shouldn't matter whether he was a player or not. This wasn't going to develop into an actual relationship. In fact, him being a man-whore might actually help me hone my flirting skills better. Hmmm...I wasn't sure how I felt about his potential reputation. Did I want him to be a player or not?

"Okay, here we go. Hot chocolate with whip for you, black coffee for me," Ivan said as he sat down at our table with our drinks. He was positioned just to my right, his knee touching mine under the table.

"Wow, really getting adventurous with that coffee order, Ivan," I said smirking. I willed my brain to focus and not let that knee distract me, even though I wanted my hand to join the party down there and really feel around.

"Well you know, I'm a guy and I drink guy coffee," he said with a shrug and a teasing smile.

"I didn't realize men couldn't enjoy variety in their coffee orders without forfeiting their man-card," I replied wryly. Okay, this was working. I was actually flirting and teasing without tripping over my own sentences.

"You make a good point, I admit. I guess I like to keep things simple. I like to eat healthy so I can perform my job to the best of my ability. That matters to me more than some triple shot, double whipped mocha frap concoction," He'd lost the teasing smile and looked dead serious. Those blue eyes stared off into nothing for a minute, making me wonder for the first time if maybe there was a lot more behind that happy exterior. The possibility intrigued me more than the hot body. There were hot men everywhere, but finding one with depth? That was the jackpot.

"Sounds like your job is super important to you, if you'll forego the bliss of whipped cream. How long have you been a lifeguard?" I wanted to know more. I took the first sip of my hot chocolate. Subpar really, but what could I expect from a national chain hot chocolate? Good to know I kicked the competition's ass though.

"Not much to tell. I've been ocean lifeguarding since high

school. I finished my EMT training a few years ago so I'm now a Marine Safety Officer, getting the necessary experience to be a Lieutenant in the next few years if certain people end up retiring as planned. I see myself doing this gig for as long as I can. Which means I need to make sure I'm in good shape," he explained, picking up his black coffee. His eyes had cleared and his bright smile was back.

"The black coffee/health nut approach is obviously working for you." I gave an appreciative glance at his upper body. "I'm glad the lifeguards out there are dedicated to keeping me safe while I just enjoy the beach. I admit, it was comforting to know yesterday that help was readily available. You're good at what you do, Ivan," I said with genuine appreciation.

"Thank you. My job means a lot to me." He paused then changed topics abruptly. "So, let's talk about you. What do you do? Where are you from?" Those eyes were pinning me with a stare I couldn't look away from even if I wanted to. Interesting. He didn't want to talk about himself. Definitely a story there but I'd give him a pass for now.

"I was actually born and raised here in Huntington Beach. I love living right by the beach. It's like my ultimate happy place. If anything's bothering me, I just walk along the ocean and I'm calmed by the sound of the waves: the crash, the hiss, the rhythm of it all. I don't think I could ever move somewhere that wasn't near the beach. I even went to college in San Diego simply because it was far enough away from home but also kept me near the ocean. So it made sense to come back here right after college."

"I know exactly what you mean. The beach is definitely my home too." Ivan paused, then the look in his eyes intensified. "I'm going to assume you're not dating anyone or else you wouldn't be here right now with me. Is that correct?" He kicked the stare up another notch and leaned even further in, now only a few inches from my face.

I was no expert, but this felt like we were leaving the flirting zone and entering a more serious conversation.

"No, I'm not seeing anyone right now. Haven't been for a while, actually. I'm not really looking to get involved with anyone at the moment," I rambled on nervously. "How about you? Seeing anyone?"

"No. I'd like to be seeing you, but it sounds like it might take some convincing," he said in a low voice.

"Well, um-" I stammered. He was straightforward, that was for damn sure. My eyes darted around as if the perfect response could be found written on the wall.

"That's okay. You don't have to say anything right now. Just know I'm interested and I'll do my best to convince you to give me a try." He paused, looked down at his hands and then back up as we locked eyes again. "I won't play games with you. I haven't been seriously interested in anyone in a long time. I don't mind waiting for you to be on the same page." He shifted so his hand was on mine, stroking my skin with his thumb, destroying my ability to concentrate on all the reasons I should push him away.

"I-I don't really know what to say to that. I'm flattered but I don't think you should wait for me or anything. I totally meant it when I said I wasn't interested in dating. You seem great, really great, and under different circumstances... But it's just not a good time for me," I hedged. I really was conflicted. He seemed sweet, he was crazy hot, and it felt like there was real substance under that gorgeous exterior. But I'd promised myself to focus on my business and not get veered off track by a handsome face ever again. I had to remember my true goals.

"No problem. We'll just get to know each other then. As friends. You can be my friend, right?" He was still stroking my hand, in stark contrast to his words.

"Sure, I can definitely do that," I replied, grabbing onto the lifeline he extended to me. 'Friends' was safe. I withdrew my hand under the guise of taking another sip of my hot chocolate, breaking contact to get my hormones back under control.

"Okay then. I'll call you tomorrow. And if you're on the beach today, I'll be at tower seventeen again. You know, if you want to stop by and say hi. Minus the jellyfish this time." He smiled as he rose from the table.

I stood up too and grabbed my bag. "Will do," I said with an answering smile. I had survived the non-date and made it clear to him I wasn't looking for a relationship. And I even got in some flirting. I was calling it a win.

He grabbed me into one of his big hugs again and this time, I allowed myself the luxury of relaxing into it. And it felt good. Like stay-for-awhile good. Like let my hands explore his back while I pressed tighter into him good. Which is crazy-talk because we'd just agreed to remain friends. Which means feeling him up would definitely send the wrong message.

Before I could explore my conflicted thoughts and decide which way I'd go, he released me, spun me around toward the exit, and kept one large hand on my lower back as he walked me out. He was a dedicated toucher. And I was starting to think I liked it.

Strictly as friends, of course.

As it turned out, I never got a chance to visit Ivan on the beach that afternoon. I had a chocolate emergency at Chocolate Dreams. One of the larger vats that stirs the hot chocolate decided to stop working out of nowhere. We had to transfer the hot chocolate to multiple little vats and then I had to tinker with the big vat to see if it was fixable. I found the problem and got it working again with the help of YouTube DIY videos. But my afternoon was shot, and all I wanted was to leave the shop in my trusty employees' hands and head home to my bathtub.

When I got home, Bailey was waiting for me at the front door.

"So? How'd the date go this morning with Mr. Lifeguard?" She was nearly jumping up and down with excitement.

"Well geez Bailey, let me put my bag down and have a seat first, huh?" I was totally joking, but played it off like I was annoyed. Because I knew it would annoy her. See how our friendship worked?

"I'm so sorry for caring so much about you." She looked contrite.

This too was an act. She wasn't sorry at all. In fact, I'm surprised that she didn't "coincidentally" happen to be at the same coffee shop this morning when my date went down. Thank God for small miracles. I knew she was just looking out for me though and I loved her for it. Time to put her out of her misery and spill.

"Okay, so first off, may I just say that Ivan is totally handsy, in a good way. I think he was touching me in some form or fashion for ninety-five percent of our conversation. He gives warm, cozy hugs. He's a health nut. He's crazy serious about his job. I'm in love with his eyes. And we decided to just be friends," I finished in a rush.

"Wait, hold up! Sounds like you guys had a great first date. Why the hell would you decide to just be friends?" Bailey had the most hideous expression on her face. Looked like 'friends' was a four-letter word in her mind.

"First of all, it wasn't a date. He flat out said he was interested in me. And I told him I wasn't looking for a relationship with anyone. He accepted that and then said we'd be friends. I really think that's for the best, Bailey." I paused. "After Jackass-who-shall-not-be-named, I need some time to wade back into the dating scene. And there would be nothing slow about dating Ivan." I started to pace the living room. "He's intense. I mean, we only talked for a few minutes and he was already saying he wanted to date me. Come on! That's way too fast."

"Hmm, I see where you're coming from, but I didn't get any weird vibes about Ivan. With Jackass, I didn't like him right from the start. Besides, it's been long enough. You need to get back out there and find Mr. Right." Bailey was speaking so calmly, like this wasn't a big freaking deal.

"I'm not ready! I'm still building my business. I wanted to wait at least another year or two before dating anyone." My voice was rising as I explained how the timing couldn't be worse.

"You can't live life according to some weird timeline you've created." Bailey waved her hand as if that objection was already resolved. "I really think you should give Ivan a chance, honey. Think of it this way, if the whole Jackass thing hadn't happened, would you be giving Ivan a shot?"

That stopped me in my tracks. It was all too easy to picture what my life would look like right now if I'd never been burned so badly by an abusive boyfriend. "Yeah, I probably would jump at the chance to be with Ivan, but that doesn't change the fact that I'm older and wiser now. I refuse to get involved with someone like Jackass again, or be distracted from my business dreams."

"I know, I believe you. But lots of women run successful businesses while in a relationship. They're not mutually exclusive. And just think on this for a minute. If you don't allow yourself to date Ivan and get to know him, you're letting Jackass still control you," Bailey said softly.

God dammit, I hated when she was right. "I'm just scared, Bailey," I whispered.

She pulled me into a hug. "I know, honey. And it's okay to be scared. But it's not okay to allow it to run your life."

And that right there is what kept me up way past when I usually fell asleep. Was I allowing my experience with Rylan to still control my decisions today? Or was I just wiser and more cautious? If I pushed the fear aside, did I want to get to know why those shadows periodically took over Ivan's eyes? Was it fair to assume he'd be bad for me? Wasn't that just painting all men with the same brush? I had to stop doing that at some point in my life. Bailey was right, I couldn't hide behind my fear. I'd made huge strides in my personal confidence but maybe it was time to get in a relationship and work out any remaining issues I had with trusting men.

Ivan called me that night like he said he would. I let it roll to voicemail. I was just too confused to handle a flirty conversation. Of course, after he left a message, I listened to his sexy voice twice before saving the message for future obsessive listening.

Hey Esa, I missed you this afternoon. No beautiful damsel in distress to carry. I know we decided to just be friends right now but I'd still like to see you again soon. Friends see each other often, right? So. Dinner tomorrow night? Call me back and we'll set up the details. Good night, gorgeous.

Good God, that man. He was seriously making me rethink my stance on dating and I'd only met him yesterday!

4

*T*he next morning, I woke up early and decided to head to the gym. Nothing like lifting some weights to clear out your brain and get you focused. I threw on some Lululemon capri leggings, my bright orange Nikes, and a muscle tee from my favorite bar in downtown San Diego. The hair got thrown up into a high messy bun that said 'I mean business'. On the way out the door I grabbed my keys, my phone, and my headphones. Time to smash some weights.

One of the greatest things about Huntington Beach is that it's a total bike town. I rarely used my car, unless I was going to work in my one of my dressier business outfits. Everything I needed was close enough that I could just hop on my beach cruiser and ride. My bike was sea foam green with a white seat and handlebars. My tires had thick white walls and my front basket was matching white. The bike's flair came from the coconut shell drink holder and the many stickers adorning her fenders. She wasn't fancy, but she was all mine.

I cruised through my residential neighborhood and then headed to the 24-Hour Fitness by my house, locked up at the bike rack out front, and headed inside. I connected my headphones, found my favorite playlist, and walked on the treadmill to warm up. Today would be an upper body day I decided. I was focused on building the best arm muscles I could. I mean really, what accessorized a tank top better than a sculpted arm? And showing off the guns was an effective propellant to douche-bros who weren't worth my time. It took a confident man to date a strong woman, both physically and emotionally. Might as well filter out the non-contenders right from the start.

Well, if I started dating, that is.

I was three reps into some overhead presses out on the weight floor when I felt someone close to my right side. I glanced over and almost smashed my head with a dumbbell when I saw it was Ivan. I put the dumbbells down and took my headphones out of my ears.

"Hey, what are you doing here?" I was already out of breath. From the weights or seeing Ivan I wasn't sure.

"I work out here too. This works out great. I was hoping to talk to you this morning." Ivan was smiling from ear to ear. Like a true gentleman, he made no mention about me not calling him back last night.

He was deliciously sweaty, the kind of man sweat where you want to run your finger along damp skin, not the gross dripping on the floor kind. He grabbed me into one of his signature hugs and I found out he smelled delicious too. A potent mix of male sweat and cologne. I missed his sunblock smell though.

His man-smell must have overwhelmed my olfactory senses. I

blurted out, "Actually, I was going to call you after my workout. I got your message last night, and I'd love to have dinner with you if the offer's still on the table."

He released me slowly. Well, released me from the hug, though he kept both of his hands on my arms. I'm sure he was impressed with my bulging biceps.

"Hell yes, it's still on the table. How about I pick you up at six and we head over to Sushi on Fire? Wait, do you like sushi?" His expression turned from excitement to concern.

"Yeah, I love sushi. And six will totally work. But why don't we meet at the restaurant? That way you don't have to come get me." I'm sure I was confusing Ivan, I was even confusing myself. Agree to dinner, but then push him away by not wanting him to pick me up. My waffling was annoying. I needed to make a damn decision.

"I'll come pick you up. I want to spend as much time with you as you'll let me, so please just let me pick you up, Esa." His pleading look won me over and I conceded with a nod.

"So, that's settled. Wanna work out together?" He looked eager to spend time with me. I was beginning to wonder how he was so good at changing the subject and the whole sunshine routine. No one was that happy all the time.

"Sure, but you look like you're already done. I was just getting started on some upper body stuff." I bent to pick up my dumb-bells again. I could have sworn I caught him checking out my butt when I straightened up. But if he was, he hid it well by looking in my eyes and carrying on the conversation.

"Nah, I just did some running on the treadmill. I'd love to do some upper body work with you. Here, I'll spot you on your over-head presses," he said while moving behind me. Good God, that would be beyond distracting. He put his hands on my wrists when I lifted the weights into position. Meanwhile, his chest was brushing up against my back and I could feel his breath raise the hairs on the back of my neck. My body was all too aware of exactly where he was.

Thank the Lord I didn't have my heart rate monitor on today. That would have been embarrassing. Just standing there barely touching and I was in the red zone.

We managed to get through a fairly tough workout together. We mostly taunted each other playfully and ended up laughing quite a bit. We both flirted by brushing up against each other or touching a shoulder here, a hand there. The man was silly, flirty, and respectful; basically, the best workout partner a girl could ask for. And then to have an upfront seat to his muscles flexing? It was straight up foreplay disguised as a public workout.

I'm sure I burned enough calories to have two hot chocolates today.

We parted ways after I gave him my address to come pick me up tonight. I had to get moving if I wanted to get home, get cleaned up, get to work, and then have enough time to get all dolled up for our date. Yes, I was calling it a date now, at least in my head. Progress!

Ivan was a few minutes early to pick me up. He pulled up to the curb in front of my house with his big white truck. I watched him park from my bedroom window upstairs. His truck looked like a manly man truck, no flashy chrome to take it out of its utilitarian-only look. He hopped out, slammed the door, and walked around the front to come up to my door. He had on dark wash jeans and a button down, black, short sleeve shirt that hugged his biceps nicely. His hair looked like he'd just taken a shower and tried to tame his unruly blond waves. He looked good.

I glanced in the mirror to make sure I looked like a girl pretty enough to be out on a date with him. No way in hell was I going to be looking frumpy while he looked that hot. And come on, two out of the three times we'd seen each other, I'd been a sweaty mess. Time to show him I had game.

I had on skin tight, dark wash skinny jeans that accentuated my booty to perfection. Do you know how many pairs of jeans I had to try on at the mall before I found the exact pair that fit my booty and also fit my waist? I don't know who's designing jeans, but clearly, they have never hit the weight room for a set of squats.

I had on a new pair of high heeled wedges, cork heel with black strappy things all over that hid any remaining redness from the jellyfish sting. The wedges boosted me up three inches from my already tall 5'7", but I would still be shorter than him. A deep blue, flowy sleeveless shirt was covered up by a faux-leather bomber jacket. My blonde hair was freshly blow-dried and curled into natural beachy waves that were the product of at least thirty minutes of curling iron hell. My make-up was on point with a perfect winged eyeliner and smoky shadow. I looked good.

The doorbell rang, breaking me out of my trance. I finished putting on my lip gloss, grabbed my small bag, and hurried down the stairs to get the door. But not too fast because these damn wedges were higher than I was used to. Hell, anything taller than a flip flop was taller than I was used to. Plus, the top of my foot was still a little sore, so I was taking it easy.

Bailey was working, which left me alone in the house with Ivan. I wasn't sure yet if that was a good thing or not. Part of me felt like I needed a chaperone, or at least a third party to make sure Ivan was a good guy and not an asshat. I wasn't quite ready to trust my instincts a hundred percent yet.

I swung open the door and smiled up at his handsome face. "Hi, come on in." I waved him inside.

He stepped into the house with a small box in his hand. I glanced down at it, wondering what it could possibly be. "I wanted to get you flowers, but I wasn't sure that would pass the "friend" test. So, I come empty-handed. This box was on your doorstep." He handed the box over and then swept me into a hug. I anticipated his classic move this time and made sure I hugged him back. Not only did he look gorgeous, he smelled damn fine too. This time, a sexy mix of soap and the same cologne as before. Mmm...more manly man smell.

"You look absolutely beautiful, Esa. You look beautiful every time I see you, but tonight...you're beyond beautiful," he said softly and with what sounded like admiration. This man and his straightforward comments were certainly having an effect on me. He swept his hand down my arm, seeming reluctant to end the contact.

"Thank you. You don't look too bad yourself." I felt my cheeks start to flush and hurried to take the box from his hands to shift the focus away from myself. I wasn't used to such close inspection and admiration, and quite frankly, didn't know how to handle it. The pit of my stomach had a weird fluttering sensation going on, which made me uncomfortable and curious all at the same time.

I inspected the box, finding only brown cardboard and clear shipping tape. The package wasn't addressed or stamped by the post office so I wasn't sure how it even got on my doorstep.

"That's odd. I wonder who it's from. I don't recall ordering anything recently." Which was another small miracle. Amazon Prime was addictive as hell. "Do you mind if I open it before we go?"

"No, of course not," Ivan replied.

I started toward the kitchen, gesturing for Ivan to follow me. I set the box on the island countertop, grabbed a knife out of the butcher block, and slit open the tape. I set the knife down, opened the flaps, and lifted out the tissue paper on top. I saw something black and started to lift it out of the box when I realized it was lacy lingerie.

"What the hell?" I exclaimed, dropping the material like it burned my hands.

"Is there a note?" Ivan moved close behind me to see into the box.

"No. There's nothing but this...thing," I said, at a loss for words. "Who would send me lingerie?"

"I promise it wasn't me. If I wouldn't even bring you flowers yet, I certainly wouldn't bring lingerie. Are you sure there's no one else that would send something like this to you?"

I saw the serious look in his eye and knew he didn't take this lightly. I didn't want him to think I lied about not being involved with someone. He had been upfront with me and I wanted him to know I was giving him the same respect in return.

"I haven't dated anyone seriously in five years! Yeah, I've been out on a few casual first dates, but nothing that would even remotely give a guy the idea to buy me lingerie." Belatedly I realized I'd just revealed how limited my dating life had been. Hopefully, he'd skip over that part.

"Five years?" Ivan's jaw dropped open and he seemed confused.

I guess he didn't miss that part.

"Yeah. It's not really that big of a deal. I already told you I wasn't looking for anything serious in the relationship department. I've got a business to run, and that takes my focus right now," I said in my defense, one hand on my hip, ready to bring out the full power stance if need be.

"Whoa, I wasn't criticizing you. I think it's great you know what you want. I'm just surprised that no guy has clawed their way into your life despite how you feel." Ivan placed his hands on my waist and dropped his head down to get eye level with me. "Esa. You've got to know how beautiful you are." His eyes were both warm and hard, taking my focus away from the creepy lingerie. He was drilling into me with that stare of his and, along with the softness of his face, led me to believe his sincerity.

"Can we just forget about this box and enjoy our evening together?" I deflected, releasing my anger in the face of such flattery. I was hoping I could coax him back to casual conversation. Not mystery deliveries or my dating history or whether I believed myself to be beautiful. That was way too deep of a conversation, especially for this non-date-between-two-friends-that-I-only-called-a-date-in-my-head.

He paused, holding my gaze, before he dropped his hands. "Yeah, we can drop the subject for now, but I'm putting you on notice. I will tell you how beautiful you are every chance I get until you believe it. You got me?"

I bit my lip, wondering how he caught on to me so quickly. I was flattered he thought I was beautiful, but I didn't like him seeing my insecurity so easily. Nothing to do but go along with it though. What was I going to do? Fight with him about how I was actually ugly? Um, hell no. Even my self-esteem was better than that. So, I nodded. He accepted my non-verbal answer by placing his hand on my back and steering me out the door.

5

*D*inner at Fire Sushi went great. Like, crazy great. We talked, we laughed, we flirted, we had incredible sushi. Ivan was a perfect gentleman. He opened doors for me, made sure I had the best seat in the restaurant, and asked my opinion on things. He never once looked at another woman, and there were plenty of beautiful ones, both in the restaurant and out on Main Street. He was so focused on me I was almost a little flustered. I was guessing this was how it was supposed to be when you're with a guy who's totally into you.

After we couldn't eat another healthy sushi roll (because even on a date/non-date, Ivan ordered healthy...no oil, no fried bits, no cream cheese, no eel sauce...le sigh), we decided to hunt down dessert. Because I insisted calories didn't count on a date, everybody knew that (except Ivan). I asked if he was up for a walk which he was. He even said if my feet hurt in my wedges, he'd already demonstrated that he could carry me. That would be entirely unnecessary but a sweet offer nonetheless.

He grabbed my hand and laced our fingers together as we began to walk down the street toward Pacific City. His hand was warm and seemed to transfer heat straight to that flutter in my stomach. This guy's touch was magic. I was starting to crave his hugs already and now I couldn't decide if I liked the hugs or the hand holding better.

"I know we decided to just be friends right now, but I gotta be honest with you, Esa. This feels like a date. A really good first date," Ivan said cautiously while glancing at me from the corner of his eye.

A small smile was on my face before I even knew what I'd say in response. The idea of this being a real date wasn't scary or repulsive at all anymore. In fact, it made my heart rate speed up with what felt suspiciously like longing. Maybe it was the wine at dinner, or the romantic evening atmosphere, or his big hand holding mine so tightly, but whatever it was, I couldn't hold back the words.

"Yeah, it sure does seem like a date, huh?" I grinned. I couldn't look at him yet, but I knew his gaze hadn't left my face.

"I was thinking, we don't want to confuse ourselves. Maybe for easy labeling we should just go ahead and call it what it is. Our first date." He pulled on my hand so I stopped walking and was forced to look at him. His expression was dead serious even though his words were playful.

A minor panicky feeling took off in my stomach at being put on the spot, but I could clearly feel this was one of those defining times in a relationship. I either got brave and decided to go down this path with him or I chickened out and pushed him away. The thought of going back to him not being in my life seemed intolerable. So, I pulled up my big girl panties (figuratively, of course) and decided to make the jump. I could always cool things off later if I felt like they were going too far, too fast. Right?

I took a deep breath in and then let it out, bringing my gaze back to Ivan. "Yes, let's call it a date. Our first date."

His face immediately lit up in that stunning smile of his, right before he grabbed me and wrapped me into a warm hug. I went without complaint, happy to feel his heart rate racing, just like mine.

After more walking, more hand holding, and more flirting, we finally reached the second level of Pacific City. I picked up my speed and led him to Chocolate Dreams, which was closed this late at night. Ivan looked at me in confusion. I whipped out my keys, gave him a secretive smile, and said, "I've heard they have the best hot chocolate concoctions in the state. We gotta try 'em!"

Before he could speak, I spun around, unlocked the door, and pulled him into my dream come true. I hit the lights and smiled with pride at the decor.

"What is this place, Esa?" Ivan looked around, then swung his eyes back to me.

"This is my shop. I'm the owner."

He grinned with a sexy look in his eye as he grabbed me by the arms. "Damn, my girl's a business maven." This must have turned him on as evidenced by how close he pressed his body into mine.

The warm glow intensified as I focused on how he'd said 'my girl'. Had we already gone from our first date to together-together? I wasn't sure how these things worked, but I figured I was right about Ivan not taking things slow. That made the stomach flutter come back, and I was just enjoying its absence.

"What's your favorite dessert, Ivan?" I asked, master of abrupt topic changes.

"Hmm...first place would be tasting you, which I'm hoping

you'll let me do soon, since we've decided this is a date. Second place would be mint chocolate chip ice cream." He cupped the side of my face with his big hand. His thumb stroked along my cheekbone and then grazed my bottom lip.

All coherent thought left my head. My lip tingled, and I gripped his bicep harder as I tried to get just a fraction of an inch closer to that hard body. Like a lightning bolt to the head, I now knew. Five years without sexy times was way too long. It was like being a starving person front and center at a buffet. Like Bailey entering a Saks Fifth Avenue with a charge card. I wasn't sure how much self-control I really had at that point. The switch was flipped, and I wanted a piece of Ivan.

He leaned down, his lazy grin went blurry, and he kissed me on the cheek. I felt the subtle scratch of his five o'clock shadow and my lips began to pout of their own accord when he straightened back up without giving them the attention they wanted.

"So, what are you going to make me, Esa?" Ivan asked in a clear voice, stepping away from me. He was grinning like he knew what sexual torment he left me in. That figures! He rushes to get me to admit it's a date, but then slows way down when I want that first kiss.

My eyes narrowed to let him know I knew what he was doing, and I'd go along with it, but I wasn't happy.

I walked around the counter and made my famous hot chocolate, wanting him to try it. Ivan was sitting on one of the bar stools watching me create my masterpiece. I made sure to include some peppermint in the chocolate mix, then topped it with our chilled, homemade whipped cream. Then I sprinkled both mint and chocolate shavings on top of the whip and finished it with a mint chocolate candy stick on the side. I came around the bar, sat next to him and presented him with his dessert in our signature white cups with pink and black logo.

He swiveled on his bar stool so our knees were touching,

picked up the hot chocolate, and took a sip. He closed his eyes for a moment, then put the cup down. I was pretty confident with my recipes, but I also didn't know if it was just too girlie for him. And for some reason, I really wanted him to like it. His opinion mattered, and I was more nervous than the day I opened my shop to the public.

He swallowed, opened his eyes, and said, "That is the best damn hot chocolate I've ever tasted. Way better than mint chocolate chip ice cream. Way better than Costco pumpkin pie. Better than a churro at Disneyland which everyone knows is perfection. You've literally spoiled me for every other dessert I'll ever eat."

I figured he was exaggerating a bit, but I still smiled from ear to ear at his praise. "I'm so glad you like it!"

"I don't like it, I love it. Here, share this with me."

We sipped and shared in friendly silence. Finally, he said, "You've got a little whipped cream right there," gesturing to my lip. I swiped quickly but apparently, I didn't get it because he leaned in and said, "Let me get it."

And that's when it happened.

His lips descended onto mine for a split second before his tongue licked across my lip. "So tasty," he whispered against my lips. I was a little shocked and more than a little turned on, so when he deepened the kiss by opening my mouth and using his tongue to explore, I actively participated. His hand settled on my hip, pulling me closer to him. The other hand cupped my face and slid into my hair, grabbing a handful, and tipping my face up for deeper access.

Since the invention of the kiss, there have only been five kisses that were rated the most passionate, the most pure. This one left them all behind.

Yes, I know, that's from Princess Bride but it totally applies.

I've never kissed a man and been completely swept up in it, losing all touch with time and place. We could have kissed for one minute or one hour, I couldn't have said. He finally broke off the kiss, keeping his forehead touching mine, hand in my hair, breathing heavily. I still tasted chocolate and his own unique taste on my lips and our breaths were definitely minty.

I think mint chocolate chip just became my new favorite flavor.

He brought me out of my fog by picking me up and situating me back on my stool. Somehow, someway, I'd half climbed onto his lap. I didn't have time to become embarrassed over it because he stood up, hauled me up in front of him, and spun me around toward the door. This was starting to become a habit.

"As much as I'd like to stay here all night with you, I better get you home." His voice had a sexy gravely tone to it that gave me hope he wasn't unaffected by our make-out session.

We cleaned up, turned off the lights, locked up, and walked back to his truck. He dropped me off at my house, walked me to the door, gave me a quick kiss on the lips, and made sure I was inside with the door locked before he roared away.

As far as first dates go, this one had some major highlights. But I couldn't stop second-guessing why he so abruptly ended things at Chocolate Dreams and why the chaste kiss at my door. I made a mental note to talk to Bailey in the morning and get her opinion.

I threw away the black lingerie the next morning, along with the box, in the garbage bin on the side of the house. I didn't want that reminder hanging around and I sure as shit wouldn't wear it! It made me feel a little creeped out that someone was trying to be so intimate with me and I didn't even know who it was. A little too stalker-ish for my tastes, thank you very much.

Bailey and I sipped our protein shakes together, leaning against the kitchen counters. I shared all the date details from the night before and my concerns over his toned down behavior after our kiss. She didn't seem too concerned about it though, telling me to just talk to him about it instead of second and triple guessing every nuance of the date. She had a point, but it still didn't make me feel better.

Just as we were rinsing out our cups, my cell phone rang. "Hello?" My employee, Jaz, was on the other end, tripping over her words, trying to get me up to speed with today's emergency.

"What? Are you kidding me?!" I asked as my eyes widened. I dropped the cup in the sink with a clatter and my hand came up to smack my forehead. Bailey stepped closer and leaned her head toward the cell phone, listening in. "Yeah, just hold on, I'll be right there." I hung up and ran toward my bedroom to get dressed.

"You better call me later, woman! I wanna know what's going on," Bailey yelled after me.

Today was not looking good, but at least I had something to take my mind off Ivan.

I speed walked up to my storefront and stopped cold ten feet away when I got my first peek of my pride and joy. Spray painted in black on the front window was tagged "WHORE" in all caps. A few drips of black ran from the bottom of the letters, down the window and onto the white window box. Jaz came up to me and threw a tattooed arm around me. She'd been with me since the grand opening and knew what this place meant to me.

"It's okay, Esa. I've just called the HB police and they're sending a detective right now. We'll get it reported and who knows? They may find out who did this," Jaz assured me.

"Why? Who would do this?" I asked, still in shock. "Wait, I know there are cameras all over the place. While I wait here for the detective, will you go to the main office and see if we can get access to the tapes from last night?"

Jaz gave me a squeeze, then took off toward the main offices. I was always grateful for her, but especially so right now. As a young female entrepreneur, it was super nice to know I had a kickass employee that would always have my back.

My shock was quickly leaving as I watched her walk off, a red-hot anger taking its place. Whoever did this would regret it. That's for god-damn sure. This was my childhood dream, and I worked my ass off to make it happen. No wannabe punk would come in here, deface my baby, call me a 'whore', and get away with it.

"Ms. Grant?" I heard from behind me.

I spun around to find a Huntington Beach City Police Detective standing with his hand thrust forward, waiting for my confirmation. I shook his hand and gestured behind me.

"I've got a little problem here, Detective," I said, sarcasm thick in my tone. A part of my brain registered that standing before me was a seriously hot guy in uniform, but I had bigger problems to deal with so I was able to keep my focus.

"Yeah, I see that. Let's have a seat over here and chat while Officer Smith collects any evidence that may be left behind," He moved toward the benches outside the shop. An older officer walked into Chocolate Dreams with gloves on, ready to take pics and whatever else the police do on a vandalism call. I sat down on the bench, but couldn't get my eyes to move away from that spray paint. Why would someone write 'whore' on my window?

"So, when did you close up shop last night?" the detective asks me with a small notepad and pen in his hand.

"Well, Detective Ramirez," I started, finally looking at the detective and eying his name badge. "We closed officially at 9p.m. but I came back in with my date at 10:30. I made him a hot chocolate and then we left around 11:00, I think." My anger was still simmering, and I was doing all I could to hold back on the sarcastic, nasty comments that wanted to come out of my mouth. It wasn't the detective's fault. I needed to be polite, so he'd work my case.

"And who was your date last night, Ms. Grant?" he asked with a small smile on his handsome face.

"I was with Ivan Whittington." I didn't think that information was really relevant, but it must be if he was asking. My eyes narrowed as I waited to see what that had to do with anything.

"I know Ivan. He's with the lifeguards, right?" he said with an even bigger smile. It was at that moment I realized that Detective Ramirez had the most mesmerizing dimple on one side of his mouth when he smiled full out. Oh great, now I couldn't get my traitorous eyes to stop staring at that dimple.

At my distracted nod he added, "He's a good guy." I smiled in response, bringing my eyes back up to his. I willed my eyes to look away from the dimple and focus on the conversation.

"Do you know of anyone that has a personal issue with you or your business? Anything else been odd recently?" Detective Ramirez asked.

I was about to automatically answer no to both those questions, but then I stopped myself. I had that weird box with lingerie delivered the other day. That was definitely odd.

"If you consider an anonymous box on my doorstep with black lingerie in it and no note to be odd, then yes, I've had something odd happen recently." A feeling of dread was taking hold of me as I wondered if the two things are related.

"I guess that depends on you. Do you frequently have lingerie delivered by secret admirers?" he asked with a raised eyebrow.

"No!" I exclaimed. "I hadn't even been dating for a long while before Ivan, so I don't know who it might be from."

"No return address? No post office stamp? Nothing but the lingerie?"

"Nothing. Totally random and out of the blue with no way to trace who it came from."

"Okay, let's talk again after I review the tapes from the

cameras they have here at Pacific City. I'll officially document this incident. If there's anything to go on from the tapes, I'll let you know. If anything else happens that seems even slightly odd, please call me on this number, Ms. Grant." He handed me a business card.

"Sounds good. And call me Esa, please." I took his card and stood up. Hey, I knew about his dimples and he knew about my lingerie and dating habits. We'd graduated to first names.

"You got it, Esa." He stood also and gave me a look that seemed extremely friendly based on the dimple on full display. "But only if you call me Jack."

What was up with all the hot men recently? I have a long dry spell and then they all come out of the woodwork! "Thanks again, Jack." I turned toward my shop and squared my shoulders at the site of my window. Time to clean that shit off my shop and open up for business.

What I didn't see is Detective Ramirez's appreciative once over of my body before he took off.

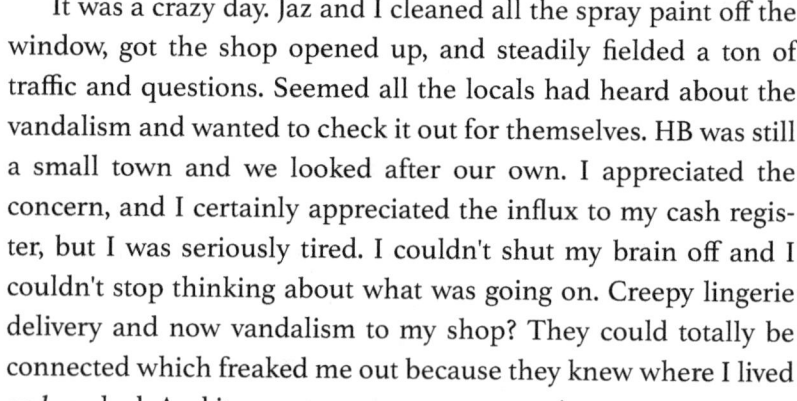

It was a crazy day. Jaz and I cleaned all the spray paint off the window, got the shop opened up, and steadily fielded a ton of traffic and questions. Seemed all the locals had heard about the vandalism and wanted to check it out for themselves. HB was still a small town and we looked after our own. I appreciated the concern, and I certainly appreciated the influx to my cash register, but I was seriously tired. I couldn't shut my brain off and I couldn't stop thinking about what was going on. Creepy lingerie delivery and now vandalism to my shop? They could totally be connected which freaked me out because they knew where I lived *and* worked. And it meant someone was targeting me.

I was stocking up our white cups at the counter when I heard Jaz mutter, "Well hello, handsome" next to me at the register. I jerked my head toward the door and made instant eye contact with Ivan. He was frowning and throwing off a seriously pissed off vibe. The line of guests waiting to place their order with Jaz parted for him as he approached the counter, as if they didn't want to mess with him and his black cloud either.

When he reached the other side of the counter right in front of me, he placed two hands down, leaned forward, and got in my space. "A word, Esa?" he growled.

"Sure," I responded carefully. No one moved a muscle and there was an awkward silence in the shop.

"Outside, please," Ivan growled again.

Oh, great, now Ivan was mad at me? Why didn't we just add that to the flaming pile of crap this day was turning into? I was called a whore on my storefront today and now Ivan was here to yell at me? Oh, hell no.

"Okay, but you can't growl at me. I don't like that tone and I've had quite the day already. I don't need you yelling at me." I didn't want to make a scene in my own shop, but I wasn't going to let him talk to me like that. I still had a big knot of angry in my belly from the vandalism. I didn't want to take it out on Ivan, but he needed to back off. No way was I going into another relationship with a guy that thought he could steamroll me. Best get that straight from the beginning.

Ivan inhaled sharply, leaned back, and smoothed his face out. Gone was the aggression, replaced by a look of concern and what I thought and hoped was respect. "Understood."

We kept eye contact, but both turned and walked out the door into the courtyard area of the shopping center. He laced his finger through mine on the way out the door and offered me a seat on the same bench I had sat on earlier with Jack, the delicious detective. Ivan settled my hand on his leg and stroked his thumb across my skin, trying to soothe me, probably. And, damn, but it was working.

"First of all, I'm sorry for speaking to you like that when I walked in. I got a call from Detective Ramirez about how your shop was vandalized and I didn't hear from you. So, I freaked out, went into protective overdrive and raced over here to see if you were handling things. Are you? Handling things?" He peered down at my face.

His ready apology smoothed over my concerns while his worried expression made that warm feeling come back. "Yes, I'm handling it as well as I can. The place has been a madhouse with people wanting to know what happened. I haven't really had a chance to sit down and rationally think about things. Jack thinks the lingerie and the vandalism might be connected. And that has me scared, to be honest," I said with a frown.

"Jack? You guys are on a first name basis now?" Ivan asked, back to that growly voice.

"Ivan, stop. Jack is a nice guy, but there's nothing there, so drop it, okay?" My eyebrows were scrunched up again. I couldn't believe he was focused on my supposed involvement with Jack when I had a serious problem on my hands. I felt like a pinball ricocheting between scared, angry, and giddy feelings about Ivan. It was exhausting.

"I'm sorry. Again." Ivan sighed, running his hand through his hair. "I don't mean to pick a fight with you. I just feel insanely protective of you and I'm saying all the wrong things."

"Well, stop making that face. You'll have major frown wrinkles if you keep that up." I reached over and used the pad of my thumb to push on the line between his eyebrows. Maybe some humor could help us both turn this day around. "Besides, I'm kind of enjoying dealing with just you right now and after a five-year dry spell, I can't handle juggling multiple men. There's nothing to worry about," I added with a teasing grin.

Ivan looked at me, his eyes still guarded. After a long moment, he sighed again and his eyes warmed. He must have realized I was being honest because his face softened into a grin right before he pulled me into him and landed his lips on mine. It was a gentle kiss that soothed me more than I could say.

"You smell like sugar," Ivan whispered against my lips. "It's distracting. I want to inhale you all day long."

I giggled and whispered back, "It's a hazard of my job."

He pulled back far enough to look into my eyes and continued the serious part of our conversation as if the sugar comment was just a stream of consciousness and not something he intended to voice out loud. "I think I should stay with you tonight, baby. I don't like that this guy knows where you live. If the two are connected, we know we're dealing with a guy totally into you sexually, and now that he saw us together last night, he's pissed off. I need to know you're safe," Ivan finished on a gruff whisper.

My heart rate accelerated. Maybe because he called me 'baby'. Or because of the kiss. Or because he wanted to stay the night to protect me. Or maybe because I was scared I now had a psycho after me. It was a lot to take in. Crazy what a difference a week could make.

Ivan misinterpreted my silence. "I'll sleep on the couch. Whatever makes you feel comfortable, but I just don't think you should be alone."

"Honestly, I'm too freaked out by what might be going on to worry about you spending the night. I think having you there would be a welcome distraction. I know Bailey won't mind either," I said quickly. If that's what it took to get him to feel like he was protecting me, then that was fine by me.

Ivan stroked my cheek. "Thank you for being reasonable. When do you get off today?"

"We don't close until nine but I have two employees closing, so I can leave any time after five."

"Good. I'll meet you here at your shop at five. We'll grab some dinner on the way home in my truck and hunker down for the evening. Okay?"

"Yeah, that sounds perfect." Then I did something I'd never done: I initiated. I leaned in and kissed him, pouring all my gratitude into the kiss. Having him with me tonight eased stress I didn't even know I was carrying. I was still worried, but it seemed like it was an easier load to bear now.

6

*B*y the time Ivan and I got back to my house that night, I was dead on my feet. The stress of the vandalism, plus the crazy flurry of customers left me wanting my pajamas and a night on the couch zoned out with Netflix. Ivan parked his truck in my driveway, hopped out, came around to my side, and helped me slide to the ground. He grabbed the takeout food bag with one hand, shut the door to his truck, and then held my hand in his. We walked to my front door, and I scrounged around in my bag for a full two minutes before I found my keys.

Ivan looked around at my house, taking in the faded brick that climbed up the bottom half of the outer walls. The top half was white paneling that matched the white columns and white picket fence that held up the front porch. I had rose bushes every-where which added a ton of color and quite a bit of charm, thank you very much. You just couldn't see them right now because my porch light either wasn't on or wasn't working. Not sure when that happened.

I heard him clear his throat right as I found my keys. A look over my shoulder showed Ivan with one eyebrow raised in annoyance.

"Esa. You can't stand out here in the dark looking for your keys. That's totally not safe. And where the hell is your porch light?" Ivan said in dismay. He looked around, shook his head at me, and hurried us into the now unlocked house. He put the food down on the side table, locked the door and flicked on the inside lights. "Do you have replacement lightbulbs here?"

"Um, I don't really know...maybe?" I said sheepishly. Home improvement wasn't my thing. Decorating, yes. Fixing, no.

"Okay, let's eat first, then I'll take inventory and see what you need done around here." Ivan moved the food containers to the dining room while I got plates and napkins.

"So, tell me about your place. This house is in a great neigh-borhood and it's gorgeous. Do you rent? Own?" Ivan began as we tucked into our Mexican takeout. Las Barcas, just a couple blocks from my house, made killer fish tacos. It wasn't Taco Tuesday, but we didn't care. Tacos were good any damn night of the week.

"Thank you. I own the house, believe it or not. My parents had paid the place off when I left for college. They died in a car accident my sophomore year and left the house to me since I'm an only child. I couldn't bear to sell it. Plus, I know they'd have such peace of mind knowing I always had a roof over my head," I said with a sad smile on my face.

Ivan dropped his fish taco, grabbed my hand tight, and focused in on my eyes. "I'm so sorry to hear about your parents. I can only imagine what that must have been like." His eyes had sympathy in them, and I squeezed his hand to let him know I was okay.

"Yeah, it was difficult. Still is. But it gets better every day, and I had my girl Bailey to help me out during the really rough parts. She was grieving too, but she was always there for me. Helped me sort out the life insurance stuff. Helped me pack up their belongings and decide what to keep. Held me when everyone's life went on after a while and I was still drowning." I had tears in my eyes now as I remembered that year. "You know it's funny, I still expect them to walk through that front door. Seems like I was just talking to them yesterday, and at the same time, it feels like I've been without them for a long time."

Ivan leaned forward and kissed my forehead, one hand stroking through my hair. "I'm sorry, baby. Death sucks, doesn't it?" He had a look on his face that made me think he knew exactly how much death sucked.

I barked out a half laugh, wiping the tears from my eyes. "That's one way to put it, yeah. But enough of that. Let's finish our tacos and then I'll take you on the official house tour." I had learned over the years that talking about my parents always hurt, but I enjoyed talking about them too. However, it was almost always a conversation killer. It was up to me to get the convo back on track.

I went to pick up my taco, but looked up again when I realized Ivan was still staring at me, frozen. I tilted my head to the side in silent question.

"You're this gorgeous, strong woman on the outside, and you've got all these deep layers on the inside. I can't wait to see them all," he said in a voice I hadn't heard before. It was soft but steadfast and held a reverence that melted some piece of my heart that had been hard and cold for too long.

There was something in his eyes, a shadow that made me feel like he understood my grief. Which really drew me in, because as a twenty-year-old, none of my friends at college had experienced their parents dying. I was odd girl out. They were all into partying and getting laid, and I was into crying my eyes out over a devastating loss, sad songs on replay. It was enough to make me feel like no one understood me.

I smiled. He smiled back. And we enjoyed the moment. We kept looking at each other, but we both went back to eating in comfortable silence.

After we finished, we threw away our trash, and I showed him the rest of my home. The kitchen, which he'd already seen, was not my favorite room since it needed to be updated and I hadn't gotten around to it, with starting my business and all. Next up was the downstairs bath and office. The office was mostly empty. It used to be filled with both my mom and my dad's stuff, but I'd boxed up most of it. It had just been too painful to see every day. I had to change the house or else I'd expect them to still be hanging out in the room. It had been hard, but I'd had to make the place my own if I was to live there.

Then we went upstairs, and I showed him the two bedrooms, one mostly empty and the other crammed with Bailey's stuff, and the bathroom. Then I opened the doors to the master bedroom and showed him my room.

When I'd decided to keep our family house after my parents died, I knew I'd have to take the master bedroom since it was now my house. But something about it didn't sit right, so I hired a contractor to gut their bedroom and redesign it so it was totally my space. It occupied the same spot in the floor plan, but it looked so different than it had growing up, that it truly felt like a new room holding only the memories I would make in there.

The bedroom double doors opened up to a view of the California King size bed. I'd decorated the room in shades of white and grey. The bed was covered in an all-white quilt with loads of white pillows. The carpet had a thick pad with a low shag, grey carpet that was crazy soft on your feet. It got cold at night and in the overcast mornings being so close to the beach. Waking up and putting your feet down on what felt like a pile of slippers turned inside out felt like a little piece of heaven. I had white plantation shutters on all the windows, which were plentiful throughout the room. I liked my sunshine. I had a few paintings and photographs of beach scenes I adored. And then came the ultimate accessory: a real life, white & blue surfboard hung on the wall above my bed. My room was kick ass if I do say so myself. Which I do, often.

Ivan looked around the space, a big smile on his face. "Rad."

Yep, that's exactly right. It gave me another happy glow inside to know he liked my personal space too. I was hoping he'd be spending more time in that space with me.

"It's time to jam-up, Ivan," I stated firmly after he'd gotten a good look around.

"What now?" Ivan grinned in amusement.

"It's time to put some comfy pajamas on. Time to jam-up," I explained.

Ivan must have thought that was funny, because he laughed, which was a really nice sound, by the way. My lips automatically lifted into a grin. He had one of those contagious laughs that make you smile upon hearing it.

Ivan hugged me. "Okay, sounds good. You get changed first while I go get my bag out of the truck."

After he left my bedroom, I had a dilemma to solve quickly. What would be appropriate to wear for pajamas? I normally slept in a soft cotton camisole with just my undies. I didn't think we were ready for that though. Besides, I intended to question him and learn some things about him for a change and I couldn't have him getting distracted by my nakedness. Plus, it was too soon for him to realize that I was, in fact, not a model and therefore had a nice belly roll when I sat down. I settled on a cotton camisole paired with long cotton pajama pants. I was just pulling the pants up when Ivan knocked softly on the door.

"Are you decent?" he called before stepping into the room.

"Just barely!" I said while my stomach went mushy. This felt intimate somehow. Wearing our pjs, talking in my bedroom. Like we were playing house together. I was nervous, but in a good way.

"Damn, I missed the show." He teased me with a half-smile, half-leer. "Turn around so I can change too. Or you can watch, it doesn't bother me."

"Ivan!" I flushed red. I turned around and heard clothes rustling as he changed pants. I walked toward my bed and climbed up on the quilt and sat down facing him, sinking a few inches into the pillows.

The red in my cheeks didn't go anywhere as I got to check him out with pajama pants hung low on his hips. His feet were bare and thank the Lord, he had nice looking boy feet. Feet weren't attractive most of the time and so many guys had nasty feet. Total deal killer. But not Ivan.

My eyes drifted back up, and I saw the sexy, male muscle bumps on either side of his hip bones. I think Abercrombie made them famous a decade or two ago. It's like they were arrows leading to the treasure. I could literally feel my lips burning as I thought about getting my mouth on them. Five years without a hint of a sex drive and I'd gone from zero to sixty in one date. I would have to turn on the ceiling fan to cool it off in here.

And then I took in the abs, and the pecs, and the biceps. All tan, all bumpy with muscle, a few strategically placed veins in all the right places. A faint scattering of dark blond chest hair tapered into a subtle happy trail, disappearing into his pants. Good God. My face burned even brighter and my eyes glazed over. That man was straight up lethal and I wasn't sure I could handle it. I mean, he was a California beach lifeguard. They made a TV show out of hottie lifeguards! He had to stay in shape for his job, he had women drooling over him all day, he took action in dangerous situations. And now he was in my bedroom, half dressed and looking at me with hooded eyes, taking in my pajama-clad self in bed.

He walked toward me and I swear it was more of a prowl than a walk. Not much to do but try to take it all in and burn it to memory. I could have jumped up and moved us to the living room, but the sexy side of me that literally just woke up from its long slumber wouldn't let me. I was frozen in place and I think Ivan knew it.

He reached the side of the bed. He lifted one leg, climbed up, and sat in front of me, knees touching mine. I could feel his heat and I was drawn to it, just like his familiar scent that surrounded me with him this close. He leaned in and touched his lips to my cheek. "Relax, Esa," he whispered against my cheek.

His words broke the magic sexy spell I'd been in. I let out a breath I didn't know I'd been holding, then smiled at him as I realized how silly I was being. We're just going to talk and get to know each other. Like an innocent sleepover or a campout. Though I'd never camped out with a gorgeous man, just the two of us. Mostly just a bunch of girls who talked about guys like Ivan. I had no frame of reference for what was supposed to go down tonight.

"Sorry, it's been awhile, as you know, and I just got a little nervous." I chuckled at myself. "Could we talk for a little bit? I feel like there's so much more I want to know about you." I laid my hand on his knee.

"I'd love to talk all night with you if you want. And I'm an open book, so ask away," Ivan replied with his trademark happiness. He moved to sit up against my headboard, tossing several pillows to the floor in the process. Then he grabbed me around the waist and hauled me up next to him, with his arm around my shoulder. I wiggled in and got comfortable with my head on his chest.

See, this is why it's a deal breaker to date a guy with ugly feet. I was lying in bed staring down at our feet out in front of us and if his had been hideous, it would have been seriously distracting. How could you possibly have a focused conversation when you had ugly feet staring back at you? And then to get under the sheets with ugly feet cooties rubbing off on my clean linens? Oh, hell no.

Dragging my eyes and my thoughts away from feet, I decided I wanted to know about more important things, like his family. "So, do you have siblings? Parents?"

"I'm an only child like you. I have two parents, still married, living in Newport Beach. I actually grew up there but feel more at home here in Huntington Beach. My parents are fairly wealthy due to my dad's business and his family's money. They sent me to good schools and paid for my college so I'm very appreciative, even though I have no plans to follow in my dad's footsteps. I can't imagine working inside all day long. It would drive me crazy to sit at a desk and stare at a wall. Thankfully, my dad's okay with my career choice. He wasn't at first, but he's come around in recent years." Ivan paused. "What else do you want to know?"

I could ask a thousand more questions about his family, because getting insight into people's relationship with their parents fascinated me and I could live vicariously through them for just a few moments. But I'd let that go for now and get into details later when I had some sleep under my belt and could better handle the emotional kick to the gut.

"Hmm...how about why you got into lifeguarding. When did you know it was the career for you?"

"Well, that's actually a sad story. I'm not sure it's the best thing for me to tell right now, considering the stress you've had to deal with today," Ivan hedged while fidgeting with my hair that lay over his hand around my shoulders.

I swiveled my face in order to see him. He was avoiding looking me in the eye, so I reached up and placed my hand on his cheek, forcing his eyes to find mine. "Hey, if you're okay sharing with me, I want to know. It's obviously important to you and that makes it important to me." Ivan always seemed so confident and carefree. So, quick to jump in and take care of me. This serious, sad side of him was something I hadn't seen yet. And I wanted to be there for him. I wanted to see all sides of him.

Ivan sighed and covered my hand with his. "Only a few people in HB actually know this story and I'd prefer to keep it that way." He paused as I nodded my understanding.

7

H is eyes stayed on mine, but lost focus as he began to tell his story. "I dated a girl my junior year of high school. Megan was her name. I'd liked her since sophomore year, but she never noticed me. I grew like six inches before junior year and took up weight lifting, and what do you know? She finally noticed me. We started dating, and it was contentious the whole time. We'd fight, make up, make out and then repeat. One night, a big group of us headed down to the beach and built a bonfire. We were all drinking, which was just plain stupid, but we were in high school, you know? So, Megan and I broke off from the group and took a blanket down to the beach where it was more secluded. One thing led to another and we had sex. It was my first time and I'm sure it was pitiful." Ivan chuckled darkly.

My stomach clenched at the thought of him with another girl, but I tried to focus back on his story as he continued.

"She was pissed that she had sand in all the wrong places and it was all my fault, naturally, so she yelled at me. I was still pulling my pants on and gathering up our things when she said she would cool off in the water. By the time I grabbed everything and made it down to the water, I couldn't see her anywhere." Ivan stopped and took a shaky breath. "I figured she went back to the bonfire. So, I went up to the group and asked where she was, but no one had seen her. I went back to the beach where I thought we'd been and I still couldn't see her. I started yelling her name, running up and down the beach, totally panicked. Our friends started doing the same. I jumped in the water with some of my buddies and we tried to dive down and feel around for her. No one wanted to call 911 since we'd been drinking, but someone finally did. Probably way too late."

Ivan rubbed his face and my heart squeezed in my chest as I realized where his story was going. Silent tears filled my eyes as I felt how much this must have hurt him, changed him, influenced him. And so young. I stroked his chest to let him know I was there for support. This must be the shadow I would see in his eyes sometimes. Why he understood death, understood grief.

"It took me a long time to get over the guilt. Hell, I'm probably still not over it. Telling her parents what happened. Telling the police. The rumors at school. It was a freak accident, but I still felt one hundred percent responsible. The 'what-ifs' just about killed me. What if I hadn't led her away from the group? What if we didn't start fighting? What if I went with her into the water?" His eyes looked haunted and so very sad.

"Leaving for college was a relief. I got away from all the people that knew, the place where it happened. I worked through the grief to realize that even though I wasn't in love with her, her loss meant something. It changed how I see life, it changed my career path. It made me who I am right now and I'm so damn grateful for her. So, I save lives for a living now, and one day I hope to have saved enough that it makes up for hers."

I knew from experience there wasn't much I could to say to make him feel any better, so I lifted up, turned fully into him, wrapped him up in my arms, and squeezed tight. Maybe all my sympathy could filter through to him and ease his hurt. I was honored that he told me his story and now I understood why he was so strict with his diet and training. It was all part of being the best damn lifeguard he could be because it would honor Megan's memory.

But what I did know was that he'd never be able to save enough lives to assuage his guilt over her death. Grief and guilt just didn't work like that. He'd need to work through that shit in his head sooner rather than later. I didn't harbor any guilt over my parents' death, but I knew grief on a first name basis. If I could help Ivan, if he'd let me do that for him, I'd jump at the chance.

Ivan turned his head and kissed my cheek. I pulled back so I could see his eyes. They had cleared, so I knew he was coming out of his story. He reached up and used his thumb to wipe the tears from the corner of my eyes.

"I didn't mean to make you cry. I'm okay, I promise. But I'm glad you know," Ivan said with a small smile.

"Is that why you freaked out earlier today? About my shop being vandalized? You know you couldn't have stopped that, right?" I asked softly.

Ivan ran his hand through his hair and took a deep breath. "I know I couldn't have stopped it, but I never could have forgiven myself if something happened to you and I wasn't there to protect you. I was too late to help Megan, but I won't be too late ever again."

"Ivan, that's noble of you, but I don't expect you to be my

protector. That's not your job. That's not your responsibility. Can you see that?"

"I don't know. Seems like, as someone who cares for you, it IS my job." Ivan paused. "We may have to agree to disagree on this one."

"I can let it go for now, but let it be noted that I disagree, huh?" I gently teased. "Maybe lay here with me? You don't need to sleep on the couch. I'd rather have you here with me." I was hopeful we could lighten the mood and find something we did agree on.

"A beautiful woman wants you in her bed, you don't ask questions." Ivan tossed an inordinate amount of pillows off the bed. "Climb in, woman." The boy looked downright enthusiastic as he whipped the covers back. I'm glad I could distract him from being sad. He was such a happy, positive person normally, hearing how upset he was in high school was hard to take in.

We wiggled under the sheets and he wrapped us up facing each other on our sides. He reached down and lifted my top leg onto his hip, placing our pelvises in very close proximity. My heart rate kicked up a notch at the intimate contact. I placed my hand on his chest.

"I promise not to push things further than you want to go, Esa. You can trust me and I'll prove it to you by respecting your boundaries. When you're ready to be with me fully, just give me a signal, huh?" Ivan went from serious to silly, bringing a smile to my face. "Maybe a bird call...can you make any bird noises? No? Okay, how about you wink at me twice? Let me see you do it."

I started laughing at the bird call suggestion. The winking I could do, which I demonstrated to his satisfaction.

"I love your laugh. I think my new life goal, along with kicking ass out in the water saving lives, is to get you to laugh every single day. You up for it?" Ivan asked sweetly.

"Oh, I'm up for it. I bet I'll find all kinds of reasons to laugh with you and Bailey around tag teaming me. Speaking of which, I need to text her real quick about you being here so she doesn't freak when she gets home from work. Do you mind?" I reached backward for my phone on the bed side table.

"Mmm." Ivan let out an appreciative moan.

"What are you-" I started to ask. Then I saw he was checking me out as I stretched out to get my phone. Sounded like he enjoyed the view. I sent him an air kiss, arched my back, and pushed the girls out a little more just for his benefit, while I began to text Bailey.

"You're killing me, woman. In bed together, a thin excuse for a shirt on, and you're posing for me," Ivan looked ready to pounce. He stroked the length of my thigh with his calloused hand as I finished up my text.

Crazy thing is, I felt perfectly safe with him. I knew he wouldn't cross any lines unless I told him he could. I don't know how I was trusting him like this after only a couple days, but it felt good and I wouldn't question it unless I saw a red flag. Though I would like to have Bailey spend some time around him. I'd ignored her opinion when it came to Jackass. I wouldn't do that this time around.

"Think you could add 'kissing in bed' to that list and still control yourself, hottie lifeguard?" I suggested with a coy smile.

"Hottie Lifeguard, huh? I like that," Ivan growled before pulling me back into his body. I'm not even sure where my phone went, but I didn't particularly care at that point. I was flush against his hard body, feeling every muscle up close and personal. His tongue was exploring my mouth, and he had my hair fisted in one hand. He rolled so I was under him and his other hand began to explore my waist, my hip, and then around to grab my ass over my pajama pants. This pushed my hips into his and I felt his hardness press into my belly. Delicious tingles ran through my body and I couldn't help but rub up against him, seeking more. It was like my body was waking up and it was in a frenzy, wanting more contact.

Ivan groaned, "Jesus, Esa" before attacking my mouth and

thrusting his tongue like I wished he would with his hips. I let my hands do some exploring of his back and then I grabbed onto his ass with both hands trying to grind up into him even more. The boy didn't forget leg day at the gym. That was some nice, tight muscle back there.

This went on for a while, legs, arms, and tongues tangling, the heat in the room rising. Ivan abruptly let go of me, rolled off, and jumped out of bed. I was still trying to get air back in my lungs, wondering where he went and why the hell he wasn't still on top of me. He stood by the bed, half turned away from me. The front of his pajama pants was tented out, so I knew he was into our make out session, but I wasn't sure why he put a stop to it.

"I gotta send a few texts, then I'll come back to bed. Why don't you try to get some sleep, okay?" he said, still out of breath, but not looking me in the eye. Then he spun around, grabbed his phone out of his bag, and walked out of my bedroom.

I wasn't sure what just happened. Twice now it'd gotten hot and heavy and he'd abruptly disengaged. Was I doing something wrong?

I turned over to my side, brought my knees up, and tried to reason out what happened. I didn't come to any conclusions. I just knew my stomach was knotted with worry. I decided to stay awake and wait for him to come back to bed so I could talk to him. It was a great idea, except I didn't anticipate how exhausted I was from the events of the day.

One minute I was laying in my bed looking at my huge portrait of the pier on the wall that I could still see even without the lights on, the next, I'm waking up with what has to be night sweats. Which would be a major bummer, seeing as how just worked my way out of a five-year sexual freeze and I'd hoped for at least a few good, active years before something crazy like menopause put a damper on my plans yet again.

Then I woke up a bit more and realized my hot flash had a name: Ivan. He was pressed up to my back with an arm thrown over me and his leg was tangled with mine. I looked up at my clock and realized it was three in the morning. I guess that conversation I was hoping for wouldn't happen, but I was happy he was at least back in bed with me. I wiggled back into a comfortable spot against Ivan, promised myself I'd confront him tomorrow, and fell back asleep.

I woke up again with what felt like twenty kisses peppering my face in rapid-fire succession. I slowly opened my eyes to a dark bedroom and a smiling Ivan propped on his elbow above me. "Hey, sleepyhead. You going to wake up so we can go to the gym before work?" His eyes were already bright and awake, but his bed head was adorably rumpled.

I considered pulling the covers back over me and going back to sleep, but I've never been woken up by a hottie lifeguard with hair I wanted to run my fingers through and twenty kisses. It's a pretty nice way to wake up.

I tossed back the covers and watched Ivan's eyes glaze over as he took in the length of me. My camisole had ridden up, exposing my stomach. My pink, lacy thong was visible above the waistband of my pajama pants. His jaw tightened and the air in the room got a bit thicker. And call me a floozy all you want, I wasn't in a hurry to cover myself up.

After his abrupt departure from our make out session last night, I was ecstatic to see I turned him on. I know I wasn't model thin and never would be, but I had worked hard the last few years to not only build a strong body, but also a strong mind that was confident in who I was. My automatic response was still to cover up and apologize for my body, which I did the first time Ivan and I met, but I wasn't going to do that anymore. He either was turned on by my body or he wasn't. And if he wasn't, well, this would be the shortest relationship in history.

Ivan dropped back down to his elbow and stretched his body out beside me. His hand traced a line from my collarbone, to the outside of my breast, down my exposed stomach, and then over the waistband of my thong. He and I both watched his hand travel, seeing his big, tanned hand on my skin being a huge turn on. Goose bumps followed wherever his hand went, the tickle causing me to catch my breath.

"Jesus, Esa. You're so beautiful. You make me want to forget about everything and just spend the day in bed with you, touching your body. Seriously. I could play for hours," Ivan whispered in that gravelly voice that instantly turned me on, knowing he was turned on.

I gave into the temptation and ran my hand through his unruly hair. "You sound like that John Mayer song...your body is a wonderland..." I sang off-tune, laughing as his eyes lit up with recognition.

"Well, I did write that song you know," he teased me. "In all seriousness, you're hot, woman, but maybe we should skip the singing, huh? How about we get to the gym and do our cardio there, not here? I made you a promise last night and I intend to keep it."

My cheeks heated as I pictured how much cardio we'd be getting if we stayed in bed. I bet Ivan was one of those guys who would take his sweet time. I'd heard about guys like that, just never been with one to verify they were real. I loved that he was being patient with me, but I kept wondering why I was waiting.

Ivan's cell phone rang as I was getting up and finding my workout clothes.

"I'll take this in the bathroom while I change, okay?" Ivan asked as he moved toward my bathroom.

I nodded and then stripped quickly to put on my workout gear when he shut the bathroom door. I was lacing up my shoes, when he came back out, disconnected with whomever he was talking to, and walked up to me.

"Esa, we have a problem," Ivan said in a serious tone. I snapped my head up and raised an eyebrow in question.

8

"What now?" I didn't really want the answer to that question. I was still processing my poor shop being vandalized, I wasn't sure I could handle more.

Ivan crouched down so we were eye to eye. "I just got a call from my buddy, Dean. He said he heard a police scanner down at Headquarters talking about a blue Honda Civic in the Pacific City parking lot being busted up. He went and checked it out. It's your car, baby. Someone busted out the tail lights, all the windows, slit the tires."

My jaw dropped open.

"Are you freaking kidding me?" I jumped up and almost

knocked Ivan down in the process. "I'm tired of this shit! Who's doing this? It can't be random, can it?"

Ivan straightened up in front of me, his hands on my arms, holding me in place.

"Let's not freak out yet. Let's go check it out, file a report with HBPD, and get you safely to work. I've already contacted my life-guard buddies. You'll be protected while you're at Pacific City since Headquarters is right there too. Don't leave your shop. I'll drive you to and from work. I'll keep you safe while the police figure out what's going on. Okay?" He dipped his head down to my level to make sure his words got through to me.

I took a couple deep breaths before I spoke. "Yeah, okay. Freak out over for right now. I just don't understand what's happening or why. Are you sure you have time to be driving me around?" Don't get me wrong, I loved the idea of lifeguards protecting me, but that's no way to live life. And I didn't want him hanging with me out of obligation either. He'd already spent the night at my place just so I'd feel safe.

"Hell yes, I have time. And why wouldn't I want to hang out with the sweetest, most beautiful girl I've ever met?" he added before bringing me in for a hug. He kissed the top of my head and spoke softly. "I know you're scared, and I hate to see that. But you're not alone. I got you."

The tension left my body at his words, my heart melting a little more. Damn, this boy was sweet. Sweeter than my kick ass hot chocolate. And that was saying something. I rested my head on his chest and just breathed him in.

Bailey burst into the room, pulling on a robe over her paja-mas. "What the hell is going on so early in the morning?" Bailey wasn't a morning person, especially when she worked late, and in my mini-freak out, I'd forgotten to lower my voice.

I pulled away slowly from Ivan's embrace and told her what happened. "Sorry, B. Ivan's buddy just called to tell us my car was trashed at Pacific City overnight. I gotta go talk to the police and then get over to the shop."

"Ah honey, this is getting ridiculous. Do you need a ride to work?" Bailey pulled me into another hug.

"I can take her this morning, but will you be home tonight, by chance?" Ivan asked Bailey.

"Yeah, I only have one client today at noon, so I'll be home after that. Whatcha need?"

"I thought I'd bring her home after work and we'd all have dinner. But then I gotta go back for a team meeting at seven. I don't think she should be alone, so will you stay with her?" Ivan asked Bailey.

"Yeah, of course! We'll have a girls' night in, just like the college days, whadya say, Esa?" Bailey asked turning to me.

"You don't need to entertain me in my own house, Bailey," I rolled my eyes. "But I do think your idea sounds fantastic....so...yeah, count me in!" I continued, building with excitement. "I'm thinking Chinese takeout, then pedicures and hot chocolate. Sound good?"

I got smiles all around so I took that as a yes.

"Another thing I like...always finding the silver lining..." Ivan muttered to himself as he went to grab his bag and get his work clothes out. Bailey and I shared a smile before going our separate ways to get dressed in our work clothes.

Time to turn this day around.

Seeing my jacked car was in my top ten 'not good moments', right behind my shop being vandalized. Whoever did it absolutely trashed it. It wasn't my dream car, but it was mine. And I'd had the windows tinted two years ago, you know, the ones that were now smashed.

Thankfully, the police finished with their pictures and finger-printing so I was allowed to get in the car and get my personal items. I had a mix CD in my stereo my mom had burned for me while I was away at college and even though the music was way old, it was from my mom. It was precious. I breathed a huge sigh of relief when I got my hands on it. Oh, and Bailey had left her latest choker in the center console so I got that out for her too.

I talked to Detective Ramirez, scratch that, I talked to Jack. He was just as good looking today, and I noticed Ivan got a little standoffish when we were talking. He wasn't rude, but he wasn't his usual happy, warm self either. Note to self: talk to Ivan about this jealousy thing again. I didn't like it one bit.

Then I called my insurance company and gave them all the police report information they needed to file a claim. They said they'd handle sending out a tow truck and getting an estimate on repair costs. I'm sure that bill would be a fun number. Mama needed to sell some more hot chocolate.

After all that, I said goodbye to Ivan with another sweet kiss, made steamier by Ivan, probably because he knew Jack could see us. I finally made my way to my shop, where Jaz was holding down the fort. Jaz had to get us lunch to go and bring it back for me since I wasn't supposed to leave the shop. I made it through the rest of the day without incident, which I considered quite good given my recent record.

Twice, a lifeguard came in to buy a hot chocolate. Which was odd because I'd never seen a lifeguard in my shop before. Did Ivan spread the word about my shop? Or about me? Or maybe he sent them to keep an eye on me? He did say he'd already contacted his lifeguard buddies, but I didn't know what all that entailed. I'd add these questions to the list of things I'd have to ask Ivan tonight. Along with finally having the discussion on his hot/cold routine.

Ivan came right at five to pick me up and take me home. I first had him haul a five-gallon jug of my S'mores hot chocolate, along with a case of marshmallows and graham crackers for dipping, to the Lifeguard Headquarters so they'd have a warm treat when they had their meeting tonight. Ivan said that was completely unnecessary, but the way I saw it, if his lifeguard buddies were sweet enough to look out for me while I was dealing with my little situation, then I could pony up some sweet treats for them in return. Ivan shook his head and shrugged his shoulders but hauled it over for me just the same.

Besides, I knew my hot chocolate. Once they got a taste, they'd be back in my shop for more. I may be in a stalker/vandalism situation but I was still a businesswoman. I had a job to do and new car windows to pay for.

After that, we went home, and dug into the Chinese food Bailey had picked up from Sully's, a neighborhood favorite of ours. We all sat around the dining table talking about how Bailey and I met, some ridiculous moments from our college days, and then our favorite places here in HB. Ivan and Bailey seemed to get along just fine, which was a huge relief. Conversation was easy, there was lots of laughter, and we were surprised we hadn't run into Ivan before the other day at the beach, given we frequented a lot of the same places.

When Ivan went in the kitchen to grab more wine, Bailey looked at me and gave me an excited two thumbs up. Silently I raised my eyebrows back, making sure she really meant it. She smiled and nodded her head firmly. I'm sure we'd discuss everything in detail later, but just knowing her judgement of Ivan's character was positive, made me feel so much better about moving forward with him and seeing how things went. I was starting to trust myself more, but my bestie's opinion was still helpful.

Ivan eventually had to leave to go to his meeting. Before he left, he dragged me into the front room to 'say goodbye' which as it turned out was code for 'kiss me up against the wall and feel me up without an audience'. Once he went out the door and I'd put my shirt back in place, I found Bailey in the living room.

We finished up the wine, put a good movie on, and proceeded to paint each other's toenails a bright pink color. With the weather warming up, I was getting a better tan which set off the pink perfectly. Now if I could just get a handle on the weird things happening, I could get back to my runs on the beach, followed by an hour of laying out time as we cooled off. I didn't think it odd at all that our cool off was double the time of our actual exercising. You put in the work, you get the payoff too. Forget Gym, Tan, Laundry. My west coast edition was Beach, Tan, Lifeguard.

Okay, no more wine for me.

9

*I*van came home around ten o'clock, walked right up, lifted me off the couch, and kissed me. If that's how he greeted me every time he came home, he could leave every night. I kept my arms around him as he picked me up and wrapped my legs around his waist. Bailey loudly clapped her hands like the attention grabbing hussy she was, just to get our attention. Then she excused herself to her room, laughing when my whole face turned red. Ivan just smirked and shrugged at her, like 'what do you expect?'. After checking all the locks and turning off the lights, we went upstairs and jammed up.

I crawled into bed and Ivan followed, laying on his side, head in his hand. He pulled me in next to him and nuzzled my neck, just breathing me in. "You've got a whole crew of lifeguards who think you're an angel. Had a few even give me fair warning that the minute I screw up, they're sliding in to snatch you up," Ivan said pulling back to smile down at me. Then his face got intense, his eyes soft. "I gotta say, you've had some trouble recently and yet you did something nice for a bunch of guys you've never met. That says a lot about who you are, Esa. So damn sweet...maybe that's the real reason your skin smells like sugar. Thank you for feeding my guys, baby."

And now I was blushing again. "Ahh, I'm glad they liked the hot chocolate. Although I find it hard to believe some of them want to date me just because of a cup of chocolate."

"Well two of the guys checked in on your shop today after I asked them to keep an eye on you. They reported back all right and spread the word about 'how freakin' hot' you are. And that's a direct quote. So, you've got a reputation already and the hot chocolate just sealed the deal. Hot girl who can feed you deliciousness? What's not to love?" Ivan explained with a pained look on his face.

"And did you make it clear I was all yours?" I asked boldly, my eyes darting around, nervous just having this conversation. My body completely froze, waiting for his response. I'd been so scared to even date him, I wasn't sure how he'd react to knowing I was now all in. Bailey's seal of approval was the last push I needed to mentally jump in with both feet.

Ivan tilted my head up and looked me in the eye. "I'm glad we're on the same page now. I did make that clear to them, and you are mine. I don't mean that in a scary way, but in a protect you and make you happy kind of way. I already told you I've made it my mission to make you laugh every day. And it goes both ways; I'm totally yours too."

My heart rate sped up and I felt like my chest would burst open with the happiness I felt. I hadn't been this happy and hopeful in a long time. I reached up and put my hand on his cheek. "I already know you're a good guy. I trust my intuition, plus Bailey gave you the two thumbs up. I know I initially kept pushing you away but I want to see how this goes with you and me. Sometimes I may slip back into not trusting or being self-conscious but I'll always try to overcome that. Just be patient with me, please?" I asked him softly.

"Always, baby," Ivan whispered, right before claiming my lips with his. He coaxed my lips apart and used his tongue to trace my lips before entering my mouth. My tongue met his and the kiss ignited with heat. He brought one hand up to hold my face in place, while his body shifted to lay half on top of me. My hands went around his neck and into his hair. I wanted to hold onto this moment, hold onto him. It felt so good to have the weight and heat of a man on me again. To feel connected. I'd been missing the physical touch and intimate connection and didn't even know it until now.

Ivan lifted onto his elbow, started to kiss my cheek, then my chin, my neck, my collarbone. He reached down and lifted my shirt to right below my breasts. He kissed my ribs, then paid some attention to my belly button while his hand drifted up and cupped my breast with a light squeeze. I gasped when his thumb swiped across my nipple, causing my whole body to light up.

"Mmm...I like that," I moaned. My hips lifted without thought and the scruff on his face scratched deliciously across my stomach. Ivan reared up and lifted the shirt up over my breasts, over my head, and tossed it onto the floor. My nipples tightened because of the cold air and his hot gaze. Next thing I knew, his mouth was hot on my nipple, drawing it in and swirling his tongue. I gasped as the pleasure rippled through me and all thought left my head. Everything in my universe was focused on what his tongue was doing to me. Then he cupped his hand on my other breast, rolling the nipple and driving me crazy.

Suddenly, cold air hit me like a wall and I blinked my eyes open to see that Ivan had hopped off the bed and was standing with his back to me taking deep breaths, his hands gripping the back of his hair. I instinctively covered my breasts with my arm and grabbed for my shirt. There were a few beats of uncomfortable silence, broken only by our ragged breathing as we both came down.

I struggled back into my shirt. "Why do you keep doing that?" I finally asked, letting quite a bit of frustration leek into my tone.

"What?" Ivan spun around to see my face, looking confused.

"Why do you keep kissing me like that and then ending it suddenly or walking off? Am I doing something wrong?" My voice quivered, which I hated, but couldn't seem to control it. I was finally brave enough to say something, but it still scared the crap out of me.

Ivan came back to the bed, sat down, and grabbed my shoulders. "No, you didn't do anything wrong. You did everything perfectly right. You think I don't want you?" He asked incredulously. "Feel this. Does this feel like I don't want you?" He grabbed my hand and placed it in his lap. He was hard. Like a column of steel, hard.

My eyes shot up to his face. "Then why?" I asked with tears still in my eyes. He felt so good, I didn't remove my hand. I wanted him, but I had to know he wanted me too.

"We're still getting to know each other, Esa. You haven't told me much but I can surmise your ex was such an asshole you felt you needed a five-year break from all men. That's a long time. And I know I already pressured you into dating me when you specifically stated you weren't interested in dating. The last thing I want to do is pressure you sexually. I'm not a saint and I've certainly slept with women in the past five years, but I've never slept with a woman who meant something to me. Not after Megan," Ivan said in a low voice.

He reached up and held my face. "You mean something to me, Esa. I want us to be together but I won't do it unless you're hundred percent on board. It's gotta be your choice. Do you understand where I'm coming from?"

I did understand him and I think I fell for him a little more, knowing he respected me enough to put the power of choice in my hands. He was breaking off our make out sessions so he didn't lose control and pressure me into something I wasn't ready for. I could trust him, and he'd already proven it multiple times.

"Yeah, I understand. Thank you for explaining and thank you for being a man I can trust."

He pulled me in and kissed me quickly on the lips before wrapping me in one of his famous hugs.

"Why don't we go to bed, huh?" Ivan pulled out of the hug to rearrange the sheets around me.

"Sounds good, but only if you'll snuggle with me."

"It's the only way to sleep with a beautiful woman," Ivan said with a wink. Then he pulled me into his chest, wrapped his arm around me, and entwined our legs together. I had my own big jellyfish wrapping around me, except this one didn't sting, just left me with a warmth that went straight to my heart.

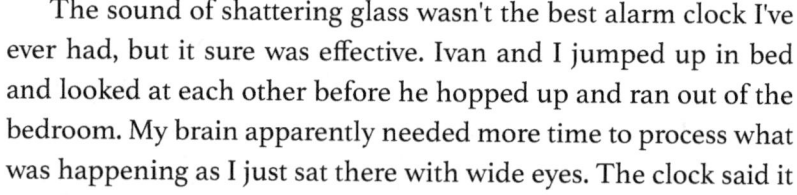

The sound of shattering glass wasn't the best alarm clock I've ever had, but it sure was effective. Ivan and I jumped up in bed and looked at each other before he hopped up and ran out of the bedroom. My brain apparently needed more time to process what was happening as I just sat there with wide eyes. The clock said it was five a.m. Glass breaking that early can never be good, right?

I shook off the sleep fog and climbed out of bed to follow Ivan. I found him downstairs in the living room at the front of the house, crouching in his boots in front of a brick and a piece of paper on the floor.

"Stay back, Esa. There's glass everywhere," Ivan barked without looking back at me.

I looked around the corner at the mess as Bailey joined me. My whole front window was shattered, the wood plantation shutters broken and hanging at weird angles, letting the cold air come in.

"Is that a note? What's it say?" I asked Ivan. My heart was pounding, and I was wide awake, seeing the damage done to my house.

He looked back at me and I almost took a step back at the anger in his eyes. "It just says 'Bitch'," Ivan bit out. He stood quickly. "Let's go in the kitchen, away from the window and call the police."

Without a hint of protest, Bailey and I turned and made our way to the kitchen. I had Detective Ramirez' card on the counter. Probably should just call him directly and add this to his ever-growing file on my drama. I picked up the phone and realized my hands were shaking. I guess being confronted with undeniable evidence that you really do have someone who hates you, and wants you to know it through acts of violence, can get through the tough exterior of any strong girl. In her typical supportive fashion, Bailey held onto me while I made the call. Ivan came back in the kitchen with flip flops for both Bailey and I so we wouldn't be stepping on any glass.

A little while later, when he and two other officers arrived in person, I gave my report to Jack, who both Bailey and I recognized looked good when he was still sleepy and fresh from bed. Ivan was in my bedroom making a phone call, leaving us to freely ogle Jack. Even in a crisis, it's important to notice the beautiful things in life.

By now it was routine: take pictures, dust for finger prints, bag any evidence. I made the officers coffee and tried to be as helpful as I could. But I really didn't have any idea who could be doing this. I wasn't aware that I'd ruined anyone's life, so I couldn't think of who might be behind this. The pit of my stomach was in knots as Jack acknowledged that this was in fact now considered a stalker case.

"This is just crazy. To think my sweet girl, Esa, has a stalker is just insane. You're the nicest, calmest, most decent person I know. How could someone treat you like this?" Bailey asked after Jack was done with his questions.

"Usually stalkers have very twisted reasons for hating or loving the person they're stalking. It's not rational which makes it hard to pinpoint who it might be," Jack explained to Bailey and I. "We'll run any prints we find, we'll keep working on the picture we got off the Pacific City cameras, and you'll need to take extra precautions to make sure you're safe. I suggest you always have someone with you and avoid highly public areas."

Ivan walked back into the room, pulling me into his side. I suppose I should be glad he didn't lift his leg and pee on me to mark his territory. Cue the eye roll.

"No problem there, Jack. Bailey and I will make sure she's always with one of us. And I've updated my supervisor on the situation. He'll make sure the team keeps an eye out when and where they can. I'll keep her safe, you find who's doing this." There was some obvious territorial macho-man thing going on based off Ivan's broad stance and his arm around me. But his tone was also respectful. Hopefully that meant Ivan knew we needed Jack's help.

"Sounds good, man," Jack replied, reaching forward to shake Ivan's hand.

Then he turned to me and gave me a hug. "I'll find this guy. In the meantime, keep yourself safe, Esa. I'm only a phone call away if you need me."

"How do I get myself a stalker? I'm thinkin' I'd like some police protection too," Bailey interjected brightly, giving Jack a flirty smile.

Everyone chuckled and Jack gave Bailey a saucy wink before leaving without offering his services to Bailey. Poor girl.

10

*B*ailey, Ivan, and I were doing our best to clean up the shattered glass on the couch, the floor, the entryway, pretty much every square foot of the first floor. It looked like a glass bomb went off, with how far the glass particles managed to travel. I wouldn't be surprised to find some shards upstairs.

As soon as we got everything swept away, and a call placed to my insurance company yet again, the doorbell chimed, announcing someone's arrival. I jumped like the floor was lava, my heart thundering in my chest as I wondered who might be at the door.

"It's okay, babe. It should just be my parents," Ivan told me as he moved to the door.

"What? Your parents?" I went from tired-but-wired to full-blown panic mode in the space of a breath. I wasn't sure what would be worse: my stalker showing up or Ivan's parents.

I whisper-yelled at Ivan, grabbing his arm to detain him, "Ivan, I'm in my pjs and my hair's a mess. And my house is a mess. I can't meet them like this. You gotta tell them something's come up. Tell them I'm sick. Tell them it's contagious. I'm puking, it's everywhere. I can't meet them right now. You seriously called your parents? Why the hell would you do that?" I only stopped to take a breath because my lungs felt like they were on fire and there wasn't enough oxygen in the room.

My absolute terror must have shown on my face. Ivan looked like he was trying really hard to conceal a smile which only enraged me more, as he got ahold of my shoulders and gave me a slight shake. "Esa, baby. Calm down."

"Oh, bad move, bad move," Bailey said from behind us. "Never in the history of men telling women to 'calm down' has that actually resulted in a woman calming down."

Ivan tossed her a dirty look over his shoulder and she threw her hands up in surrender. "I'm just sayin."

"Sweetheart, I called them and asked them to come over. My dad knows some people that do some undercover type work. He thinks we should hire them to help find this guy. Please let them help you. Just listen to what they say and give it some thought. My parents are nice people and you don't need to try to impress them. Let them in. Please?" Ivan was leaning down looking me in the face with an earnest expression. His eyes were pleading with me and I knew right then I couldn't win, couldn't resist those eyes.

"But...meeting parents is a big freaking deal, Ivan," I pouted. My shoulders drooped in defeat. I knew my face held an expression that only whiney two-year-olds make when they weren't getting their way. This was a losing battle, I could feel it.

"Please? For me?" Ivan whispered. Then he used those hands

to massage my shoulders, and I discovered defeat felt better with a massage.

He was being sweet and totally rational, damn him. They'd come all the way over here at 6 a.m. to help a woman they'd never even met before. I'd be a total bitch if I didn't welcome them in and at least have a conversation with them. The doorbell sounded yet again, jolting me out of my thoughts.

"Okay, I'll talk to them." I took several deep breaths to steady my heart rate. Ivan squeezed my shoulders and gave me a quick kiss, then walked over and opened my front door.

Standing on my doorstep was the most put together couple I'd seen in a long time. Ivan's dad was tall like Ivan, had blond hair mixed with a lot of grey, blue eyes, and a nice tan. He looked to be in good shape for his age, but had on the typical rich, white guy outfit of slacks, polo shirt, loafers, and sunglasses tucked into the V-neck of his shirt. Most importantly, he was wearing a kind smile which I took as a good sign. Ivan's mom looked impeccably put together, especially for an early morning surprise visit, with her dark blonde bob haircut, blue eyes, sweater set, slacks, and loafers. She had jewels in her ears, on her wrist, around her neck, and on her fingers. She too wore a kind smile, so I clung to that and hoped it boded well for our first conversation.

I took this all in while also wondering how to get the hell out of this situation. I was in flip flops, pajama pants, and a thin camisole, for God's sakes. I can't believe Ivan didn't give me advanced warning. Suddenly I realized everyone was looking at me expectantly.

"Um, I'm sorry, what'd you say?" I looked at Ivan for help while stepping closer to his parents. I plastered on a smile and decided 'fake it till you make it' was my motto this morning.

"Esa, these are my parents, Susan & Mitch Whittington," Ivan repeated while gesturing to his parents. He kept one arm around my back, for the dual purpose of offering support and making sure I didn't escape, I'm sure.

I immediately reached out and shook Mitch's hand with a big smile on my face. "Hello, Mitch. It's so nice to meet you," I said brightly. Then I went to shake Susan's hand, but she reached forward instead and gave me a big hug. "Oh, nice to meet you too, Susan. Now I know where Ivan gets his fabulous hugs from." They both smiled back at me and I moved back to invite them into my house.

"Sorry about spacing out there for a second. It's been a crazy morning," I explained as we moved into the living room. "Please, have a seat."

Bailey came into the room and quickly handed me my sweat-shirt as she turned and introduced herself to Susan and Mitch. Thank God for best friends and their foresight. I whipped the sweatshirt over my head, sitting next to Ivan on one couch as they sat on the opposite couch together. Bailey took the wing-backed chair. Ivan wrapped an arm around my shoulder and pulled me close, offering support, knowing I was still freaking out inside.

"Oh honey, I can only imagine how unsettled you must be feeling right now. Ivan told us over the phone some of the things that have been happening. I'm so sorry to hear you're dealing with this," Susan said, sympathy all over her face.

"Thank you, Susan. I've never had this happen before so I'm not sure how I'm feeling quite yet. I'm just hoping the police catch him soon."

"Well, that's what we wanted to talk to you about, Esa," Mitch jumped in, leaning forward with a serious look on his face. "We have a good friend who owns a private detective company that has solved some incredible cases. He's the best in the area, hands down. We think we should get him on your case ASAP. He'll work closely with the police, but let's be real here. The police can only do so much with their limited time and resources. This stalker seems to be escalating and I strongly feel we should hire this private detective before things get out of control. What do you say?"

I blinked. Then took a long breath. Then blinked again. That was a lot to take in. "To be honest, sir, I haven't had a chance to think about the best course of action yet. I'd obviously like him caught, sooner rather than later, but I don't know what a private detective costs. I'm assuming I won't be able to afford that. Besides, I'm sure the police will be able to do all the same things," I explained, while alternating looking at Susan, Mitch, and Ivan.

Ivan gave my shoulders a squeeze before leaning into me and grabbing my hands in my lap. "Don't worry about the cost of the private detective. I've got that covered. I think you should hire him and catch this guy. He's obviously not stopping and my dad's right; his attacks have escalated. I'm worried his next attack will be less about property damage and more about hurting you. I can't let that happen. Let's hire the detective and make sure you're safe."

"Bad move, bad move..." Bailey whispered from her chair. Mitch and Susan looked over at her curiously but turned their attention back to me when Bailey didn't elaborate.

I sat up taller, took a breath, and calmly explained why that just wouldn't work for me. "While I appreciate the offer, I can't let you do that, Ivan. This is my problem and I will take care of it as I see fit. I don't have the money for a private detective right now, so I'll let the police handle this," I said firmly.

I didn't want to seem rude in front of his parents, but I didn't appreciate him swooping in, throwing his money around and saving poor little helpless Esa. I'd made it this far on my own, I'd make it through this too.

"Esa, I really think you should reconsider. This stalker sounds dangerous. We just want to see you safe and sound," Susan interjected, a pleading look on her face.

"And I appreciate your concern, Susan, I really do. I'll take a look at my financial situation and see if I can swing it. If I can, you and Mitch will be my first call," I placated, hoping she'd understand my position.

After that, there wasn't much to say, so thankfully the Whittington's cut through the tense situation by announcing they had some people to meet for breakfast. I don't know if that was the truth or not, but I appreciated their tact. They took off after hugs all around and promises to come visit them for dinner sometime soon. Bailey took off to her room to get ready for work and I told Ivan I needed to do the same thing.

"Babe, why don't you take today off work. Stay home, get some rest, and try to relax. You've had a crazy couple of days. I'm sure Jaz can run things without you there." Ivan pulled me into his body. He rubbed his big hands up and down my back, which was heavenly and totally tempting. It would have been so easy to rest there in his arms and take the day off, try to forget my problems. But I was made of tougher stuff. And I had a business to run. And a life to lead. No one could do those things but me. And my stalker wouldn't change any of that.

I straightened up, pulled out of Ivan's embrace, and said, "Thanks, but I need to keep doing my normal activities. That'll help more than anything. If I sit here at home, I'll have too much time to just think and worry. Besides, I may have to hire a private detective in the future, so I better drum up some business. I've got a meeting with the property management company about running a spring event with some of the other vendors and I don't want to miss it. But I won't stay too late. I promise I won't be burning the midnight train."

Ivan burst out laughing. "Um, okay, I'm glad all the midnight trains are safe. Maybe you shouldn't burn the midnight oil either."

I cocked my head to the side and turned the words around in my head. "Yeah, that's what I meant."

He just looked at me with amusement and shook his head in defeat. "I'll drop you off on the way to work." Then he pulled me back in with one hand around my waist and the other cupping my face. "How about dinner at my place tonight? I'll cook, you can relax, then spend the night with me. What do you say?" His voice lowered, eyes becoming lazy and heated. It was a good look on him.

"Well, I can't refuse that offer. But only if you'll let me help you make dinner."

"You know, you really need to learn to let someone take care of you. I'm cooking you dinner and you can't help. You can sit in the kitchen with a glass of wine and chat with me, but that's it. I want you to relax. You got me?" Ivan had a stern look on his face.

"Yes, sir! Now may I go get dressed, please?" I asked with fake innocence. A little sass would make sure he didn't think he could always get his way. At least, that's what I told myself.

"Yes, I'll allow it," Ivan teased, smiling at me. I gave him a nasty glare before turning to go upstairs to my room. I yelped when he smacked me on my ass, spurring me into a run to escape him.

"Watch out, hottie lifeguard! Payback's a bitch..." I warned him as I ran up the stairs. I know he saw the evil gleam in my eye, but he just smiled back at me, like you would at a cute, mischievous puppy. Clearly, I would have to work on my threats.

11

$\mathcal{L}$ater that night, Ivan took me home to his place, a condo north of Main Street. It was two stories, with shared walls on both sides. The inside was decorated in sleek modern lines and grey-blue colors. It was surprisingly clean for a guy's house, but then again, Ivan wasn't your typical frat boy with a bachelor pad. He set me up with a glass of wine and a barstool in the kitchen while he made us dinner.

"It's nothing fancy, but it'll be quick. And also good for us," he told me with a wink. He pulled out a large saucepan and tossed in two bags of frozen Asian vegetable mix. He set it on the stove to heat.

"I would expect nothing less from you. Besides, I haven't been able to do my beach runs with all the craziness, so I could use a little bit of healthy." I sipped my wine, enjoying the show.

"You look damn good to me. But healthy food is good for more than just what you look like. The right food will give you good energy and strength, not to mention stamina." His look turned lecherous. Okay, seriously, before an ovary exploded, I needed to sleep with this man. My expectations were getting higher and higher, so I hoped I wasn't setting myself up for disappointment. My gut told me Ivan wouldn't disappoint.

He turned his gaze from me to the chicken breast he was chopping. He added it to the pan, covered it with a lid, then washed his hands before throwing down the towel and stalking over to me. He took my wineglass out of my hand and set it on the counter. One hand fisted in the back of my hair as he tilted my head back and kissed me. He let out a low moan as his tongue swept through my mouth. He deepened the kiss and pressed my body into his as he crowded me into the counter. I wasn't in control of this kiss as it was all Ivan. With my head tilted back and sandwiched between his body and the counter, I was at his mercy. I usually enjoyed being in control of everything around me, but his claiming me was electrifying and it turned me on something fierce.

"Hmm, I missed you today," Ivan whispered against my lips as he came up for air. Then he sniffed and straightened up suddenly. He pivoted to the stove, jaw locked in irritation. "Shit, I almost burned our dinner." He lifted the lid on the pan, turned down the burner, and tossed in some soy sauce and a splash of hoisin sauce. "You're dangerously distracting, Ms. Grant, sitting there with your hair all tousled from my kiss," he said over his shoulder with a sly grin.

I touched my fingers to my lips, feeling them swollen and definitely wanting more. I also wanted to know how he learned to casually toss the word 'tousled' into a conversation. Ivan was turning out to be an intriguing mix of typical macho male behavior and old-fashioned Victorian housewife.

I knew he was busy making dinner, but as I sat sipping my wine, I was wondering if we could go back to the kissing portion of this date before we sat down to eat. Suddenly I was ravenous, not for food, but for a taste of Ivan. I think I could feast entirely on his body. So many places I wanted to lick and nip. How far would he let me go before he put an end to it? Was I ready to take things further?

Ivan interrupted my thoughts by placing two steaming plates of chicken stir-fry on the dining table. He was looking at me expectantly, head tilted toward the waiting food. I got up and joined him at the table, realizing I must have completely zoned him out. The steam was rising from my plate, carrying the scent of the Chinese food I loved.

I took my first bite, chewed, swallowed, and grabbed his hand. I pleaded in my best throaty voice, "Marry me now."

Ivan laughed and dug back into his plate. "I'm glad you like it. Maybe you should wait to see if I can take out the trash before you offer yourself up in marriage, huh?"

"Nah, I'm easy. You can make Chinese food. I'm sold." I laughed and continued eating with gusto.

We spent the whole meal talking about our day and little things that came up at work. Ivan was a good listener and offered ideas when I asked for them. Otherwise, he just listened and asked questions. Very easily, I could see us sitting like this every night, enjoying each other's company. It was probably too soon to be thinking that far in the future, but I was taking it as a good sign. He never once told me what to do, or belittled my ideas. Already the complete opposite of Jackass.

Speaking of Jackass. As we were finishing up our meal, Ivan finally asked, "I know this is a touchy subject, but I have to ask...do you feel comfortable telling me why you had a five-year dry streak?"

Ah, the ex-boyfriend conversation. I knew I'd have to have it, I'd just been avoiding it. It was hard to talk about and I didn't want Ivan to view me differently, knowing the crap I put up with before. I wasn't the same girl anymore, but there was still residual shame that lived in my gut. I knew I had nothing to be ashamed of yet it still lived on.

"Well, it's not a story I like to relive, but I'd like for you to know. I dated a guy in college. Name was Rylan. I was still emotionally raw since it was so soon after my parents died. Looking back now, I think he could see that. He was so sweet and attentive at first. He totally love-bombed me in the beginning." I took a deep breath. "And then once he knew I was committed to the relationship, after the first night we slept together, he changed."

I brought my gaze back up to Ivan, searching his face for clues about how he might take all the details I was about to unload. "I'm not sure how much detail you want me to go into," I whispered.

Ivan ran his hand through his hair, his eyes tortured. I was sure this wasn't easy for him to hear. "I want to know everything so I can help you deal with your past. Make sure I don't do anything to hurt you, given your history." He ended with a firm nod, as if to convince himself, along with me, that he could handle the full story.

"Okay. Stop me if it's too much." I took a deep breath and launched into the ugly. "Our first time together, he was sloppy at first, then his hands pushed my head down to his lap with an obvious request. He kept his hand on the back of my head with a painfully tight grip on my hair. When he was done, he pulled me up the bed and just fell asleep. I was disappointed, of course, but wasn't alarmed quite yet."

"At some point during the night I woke up on my side with hands grabbing my hips from behind as someone rubbed them-selves along my backside. I barely got out his name before he lifted my leg and thrust into me. I remember it stung. He was thrusting into me roughly, grunting the whole time. He lifted my leg even higher toward my chest, pinning my knee to the mattress. With his upper body lying on top of me, I couldn't have moved even if I'd tried to fight it." I paused as Ivan looked down at his clenched fists, the muscle in his jaw twitching. He closed his eyes for a second, then opened them, looked back to me, and nodded at me to continue. His eyes looked guarded, but I couldn't stop now. I had to get it all out.

"He finally stopped, breathing heavily onto the back of my neck, then rolled over and fell back asleep."

"I laid there till the sun came up the next morning, wondering what just happened and why tears were sliding down my face again. That wasn't making love, that much I knew. It was rough and painful, completely one sided. And I wondered if that was how it was supposed to be. Did I want that? Was I making too big a deal of it? I'm sure I wasn't the first girl who didn't orgasm during sex. Maybe it was worth putting up with, just to keep him by my side. Because just having someone felt better than being alone. I didn't want that. God, anything but being alone."

"So, the next day I didn't break up with Rylan like I should have. I didn't even talk to him about what happened. I didn't express how I felt disappointed, or how I deserved to be treated better, or the fact that I was unhappy. I just went along with it all. Steamrolled. No backbone whatsoever."

I had real tears running down my cheeks by this point. I was sad for the girl I used to be. But I could also feel that I wasn't that girl anymore. And I never would be again.

"He got controlling. He started ridiculing me, tried to change me. Made me feel so horrible about myself. Didn't respect me at all. And the worst part is, I let him. The downward slide of the relationship after that night was easy for everyone to see, but me. The attentiveness turned into possessiveness. The loving kisses turned selfish and demanding. The sweet remarks turned into backhanded compliments to make me act, dress, and speak like he wanted. His hands still touched me, not to give me pleasure, but to grab my belly and tell me I needed to cut down on the sweets. Study sessions degraded into insults of my study habits, grades, and intelligence. I could do no right in his eyes. The scariest thing was that the abuse escalated so subtly over several months, I couldn't even see it. I knew I didn't feel happy, but I didn't see how badly I was being mistreated. It was Bailey who finally stepped in to make me see straight."

"She managed to get me alone one night and took me to a battered women's shelter to volunteer. As we served food and helped the women find an open bed for the night, I talked to the women about their situations. Imagine my shock when many of their stories started to sound familiar. Their abuse started out with just the insults and lack of respect too, quickly becoming physical in nature. One woman even told me about how she'd been raped her first night living on the streets. She was so thankful for the shelter to keep her safe at night."

"By the time we left after our shift, I just sat in the car with Bailey and sobbed. The shock of realizing that I was in an abusive relationship warred with this overpowering sense of shame. I didn't even have the good sense to walk away from my abuser when it first started that night when he all but forced himself on me. How could I have thought being alone was worse than being degraded on a daily basis?"

"Bailey held me while I explained all that was going on in my relationship with Rylan. She didn't say much except she suspected that was happening and she was there to help me end things. No judgement or wondering how I could have allowed it to happen. I don't think I could have handled her anger on top of the shame and humiliation I already felt for myself."

"I don't know what changed in my mind but as I sat there with Bailey, I decided I was done. Done with crying. Done with feeling bad. Done with being disrespected. Done with having Bailey save me from my own life. That was not who I wanted to be and if I didn't turn things around, I wouldn't recognize my own life. I loved Bailey for always being there for me, but now I needed to be there for me. It was time to grow a backbone."

My hands shook as I recalled the nightmare I lived with for several months. Ivan scooted closer to me and put his hands on mine, steadying me, bringing me back to the present where I was safe. I gripped his hands like a lifeline.

"I dumped him immediately. He didn't take it well. It was an ordeal since we went to school together. He kept trying to contact me and I was spending more time dodging him than studying. I had to get a restraining order and then I heard he transferred colleges. Never saw him again. But it took a long time for me to pull myself out of that horrible place he left me. Build myself back up. Decide who I was without his influence. And I swore to get my life together before dating again. I owed it to myself to make my dreams come true before adding someone else to my life. Graduate college, own my chocolate business. I promised myself that I would never compromise myself again."

I ended my story, gathered my courage, and looked into his eyes to see his reaction. To my immense relief, I only saw sympathy and respect shining back at me. No revulsion or blame or pity.

Ivan sat and digested my words, never taking his hands from mine. I gave him time to formulate his response, knowing it was a lot to take in. I already knew how much he hated when I talked badly about myself, so I knew he wouldn't like hearing how bad I let it get with Jackass.

He finally lifted his head and caught my eyes. "First, thank you for trusting me and telling me what happened to you. I can't wrap my head around him treating you that horribly. That should never have happened. And I'm also grateful that you allowed me to end that five-year pause. That you took a chance on me. Now I know not to take that choice you made lightly. Your story only makes me respect you more."

He paused and stared at me for long seconds. "Your parents died, your boyfriend abused you and you had to take it to the legal system to be rid of him, you started your own thriving business, you're dealing with a stalker. Esa. You're flat out incredible. So incredibly strong, stronger than anyone I've ever known."

Then he pulled me in for a hug, his words seeping in, warming me up from the inside out. Yeah, I *was* strong. I rarely took the time to recognize that fact, yet here's Ivan, only knowing me a short while and he spotted it. I was used to having Bailey in my corner, but it was looking more and more like Ivan was in that corner with me too. And even though it was scary to open up, it also felt really good.

We stayed in our extended hug for a long while, just absorbing each other. I felt a million pounds lighter having told him all that happened, like an invisible weight had been lifted off my chest and I was finally free again.

I pulled back from the hug. "All right my hottie lifeguard, you ready to move on to happier topics?" I asked him, smiling. He smiled right back, let me go, and up we stood.

I helped him clean up the kitchen and then we went into his living room to snuggle on the couch with the TV on. Ivan pulled a blanket over us as we sat with our feet up on the ottoman. He wrapped an arm around my shoulders, pulling me flush against him. His other arm rested on my stomach. We watched news for a few minutes before Ivan moved his hand under my shirt to stroke my skin and asked, "Do we really want to watch the news?" His eyes were on my lips so I could guess what he wanted to do instead. Thankfully that aligned perfectly with what I wanted to do too.

I reached up to grab his hair at the back of his head, pulled him the last two inches into me, and ran my tongue along his lips before he opened up and I took the kiss further. Then I teased him by backing off and just nipping at his bottom lip. "Mmm, I love this more assertive side of you," Ivan whispered against my lips, his curving up into a smile.

"I think I do too." I lifted a leg and climbed up onto his lap, straddling his hips so I could snuggle in closer. "I feel safe with you, Ivan." His eyes warmed by shifting into a deeper blue, his arms tightening around me.

"Always safe with me, baby. I got you."

I realized then that I would do just about anything for this guy. He was saying and doing all the right things to calm my bruised heart. I was beginning to rely on him so much, and we'd just met a few days ago! I already trusted him in a way I'd never trusted Jackass. I knew Ivan wouldn't hurt me. In fact, I knew he'd go way above and beyond to make sure I never got hurt. To finally have someone I could trust and rely on to always be there for me, well, that was what I'd dreamed about but didn't think actually existed.

I placed both hands on his face and looked him right in the eye. "I know you do, babe." And then I kissed him.

Everything I was feeling went into that kiss. I wasn't thinking anymore, this was all feeling, all heat of the moment. I pressed as close as I could get to him, my hips bucking without my awareness. My tongue tangled with his as we both fought to get as close as possible to each other. I was burning up inside and only Ivan could provide relief.

Ivan reached down to grab the bottom of my shirt and whip it over my head, dislodging my hands from his face. Any second without contact with his skin seemed too much. I threw my hands back onto his shoulders to get back to feeling his warmth. Then I slid my hands down his back and lifted his shirt up and off. My hands moved all over his torso, touching as much of him as I could.

Skin. I wanted all his skin pressed to my skin.

Ivan reached around and undid the clasp of my bra. Then he

used his fingers to trace a path, removing my bra straps. Down my shoulders, down my arms, the cups slipping off my breasts. His head soon followed, warm kisses sprinkled over my collarbone, my shoulder, around each of my breasts. Then he lifted me up and latched onto my nipple, causing me to reach up and hold his head to my breast. The way he flicked my nipple with his tongue made me squirm on his lap, wanting more but not wanting to move on either.

The room was quiet except for the television on low in the background and our groans and my gasps. Suddenly, Ivan flipped me to the right, onto my back on the couch. He adjusted so his hips were resting between my spread legs. His lips found my other nipple and gave it the same attention. I couldn't help but rub up on him as I felt his arousal press into me. I heard a mewling noise and somewhere in the back of my brain I thought he had a pet, then realized it was me making those noises, completely out of control.

I flushed as I thought about how easily I could come right now. Just his mouth on my nipple and dry humping his jeans. It had been a long time since something other than my vibrator had made me come. And even before that, all two of my previous sexual partners had been seriously lacking, if this experience was anything to go by.

Ivan left my nipples and reached down to unzip my pants, lowering them down my legs and then off entirely. As I laid there on his sofa in nothing but my blue, lacy underwear, Ivan sat back on his legs to admire the view. I resisted the urge to cover up or apologize for my body. I wouldn't bring that into this relationship. I promised myself then and there to allow him some control in our relationship. I needed to show him, and me, that I trusted him.

"You, laid out on my sofa, legs spread, your nipples wet from my mouth, just looking at me so trusting with those beautiful eyes...that's gotta be the most gorgeous thing I've ever seen. I will never forget what you look like at this exact moment," Ivan uttered in his sexy gravelly voice.

My pulse soared and I couldn't help the warm flush that spread over my body. I felt exquisite under his gaze. I felt better about myself than I ever had before. I was showing him the real me and he liked all of it. Nothing sexier than him wanting me for exactly who I was.

Then he crawled back over me and began to kiss his way down my body. Eyes, nose, jaw, neck, shoulder, between my breasts, my stomach, each hip, my thighs, my knees, and my feet. His hands massaged back up my legs and he grabbed my underwear on each side of my hips and tugged them downward. Once they were finally off, he bent one knee and propped my leg up high on the sofa back.

Reflexively, I immediately went to cover myself, but he stopped my hands, looking into my eyes. "Trust me, baby. Let me make you feel good." I smiled shyly, remembering my promise and put my hands back over my head.

I relaxed back down and he took my wrists in his hands, placing my hands on both of my breasts, silently instructing me to fondle myself. Then he dropped his head to kiss his way down my thigh, resting one hand on my stomach. He finally zeroed in between my legs, licking a long, slow line up my center. I gasped and lifted my hips. I wanted more. I had to have more. He obliged by targeting the one spot I needed his tongue the most, licking and then retreating to play elsewhere. This continued for long minutes before I couldn't stand the teasing anymore and exhaled a loud, "Ivan, please!"

"Ivan, please, what, baby? What do you want?" Ivan replied, much more calmly than I appreciated. He was in control, and he clearly loved it.

"I need to come. Please," I responded, more breathless than I wanted. I didn't care I was basically begging at this point.

Five years, people. I was desperate.

"Okay, baby. Your wish is my command." The devious smile was sexier than hell. "But I need you to play with your nipples. I'll only keep going if you remember to do that. Got it?"

I nodded vigorously and began to roll my nipples with my fingers, showing him I could follow his directions. He watched for a few moments, then he attacked me, kissing and licking and sucking with abandon. Then one finger found its way inside me, pumping in and out, along with his tongue on me. I think a second finger found its way in as I felt deliciously filled, but really, I was too far gone to tell you exactly what he was doing to me. A few more pumps of his hand and his tongue flattened, finding a rhythm on my clit and I was sent hurtling over the edge. My back bowed off the couch, my fingers left my breasts to grab his hair, and I cried out his name. My eyes were squeezed shut, but I saw stars and bright colors on the backs of my eyelids.

Eventually, as my awareness came back down to the room, I relaxed my fists and opened my eyes. Ivan removed his fingers, gave me one last kiss, which sent me jumping since I was still sensitive, and sat back on his heels. His mouth was wet from me, his hair disheveled from my fingers raking through it. He wore a proud, heated expression that he'd earned, I admit. He looked damn sexy.

"That. Was. Fucking. Amazing," I said slowly, trying to catch my breath. I was so relaxed from the best orgasm I'd ever had, I didn't even think to close my legs or cover up in any way. Maybe that was the secret to great body confidence: experience such amazing orgasms that you don't remember to be self-conscious. If it was, sign me up for more!

Ivan crawled up on top of me, draped his lower body on me, his upper supported by his arms, before kissing me. "Thank YOU, for trusting me. I don't take that lightly. Besides, I like tasting you. You're fucking delicious." He flashed a ravishing smile, which turned into a laugh as he saw my cheeks heat because of his bold words.

I could still feel his hardness against my belly, belatedly realizing that he didn't get to participate in the orgasm party. Before I could even offer, Ivan shook his head saying, "I don't want anything from you. I want to wait till I'm inside you before I come. When you're ready, I'll be ready. Okay?"

I nodded my head that I understood, realizing yet again, what a good guy I had. And to think I tried to tell him I didn't want to date anyone! Thank God, I let that fear go and gave him a shot. Now if I could just get rid of my stalker, life would be perfect.

12

he next morning, Ivan took me back to my place so I could shower, get ready, and then go into work with Bailey dropping me off. Ivan was going straight to work after promising me dinner together later that night. He waited until I was safely inside my front door before I heard his truck zoom off.

In the kitchen, I started the coffeepot and waited for the heavenly aroma to drift up to Bailey. I wanted to talk to her about everything with Ivan and I knew the way to get her down here was through her caffeine addiction. I upped the ante by pulling out eggs and cooking up cheese omelets.

I was just about to slide them onto plates when I heard her enter the kitchen.

"Yo, bitch! What's with all the early morning racket?" she grumbled as she belted her robe. The girl was still half asleep and yet she looked model gorgeous. I was always telling her she should think a little less about dressing other people for a living and get into modeling herself. She always laughed me off and said modeling would be too boring.

I tossed a dirty look at her over my shoulder, knowing she was teasing me, and deciding to tease her right back. "I made myself an omelet and some coffee. Too bad there wasn't enough for you too. Maybe next time, *bitch*."

There was silence and then she and I both broke into laughter at the same time.

"Get your ass over here. Take your omelet and coffee to the table. I wanna have some girl talk," I told her.

"So bossy these days..." she grumbled as she passed me on the way to the food on the counter.

We sat at the dining table and dug into our food. After a few bites, she looked up at me with raised eyebrows. "You gonna spill the details or what?"

"Hmm, where to start, where to start. Okay, let's start with the stalker situation. I was thinking about it, and I don't like feeling vulnerable to some psycho. And I know Ivan has been with me most of the time, but he shouldn't feel like he has to protect me 24/7. I'm a grown ass woman, am I not? So, I was doing some research at work yesterday. How about you and I take a self-defense course?" I threw it out there at her quickly. "I found a place off Main Street that specializes in women's self-defense. And I really want to take a class, but it would be a thousand times more fun if you did it with me. Please say you'll go."

She had stopped eating during my plea. She narrowed her eyes at me, paused to think, and then clapped her hands as her face cleared. "Yes! Let's do it! Just tell me when the classes are and I'll see which ones work around my schedule. I hope they teach us to kick some ass. I'd love to drop a crazy move on some guy at a club. Wouldn't that be so fun? We'd be so rad!" Bailey was nearly bouncing up and down in her chair. I was thinking I just wanted some moves to defend myself from an attacker. Bailey wanted to BE the attacker! And that is why I loved this girl.

"Okay, okay, I'll call them, run the classes by you, then book it. Second order of business: Ivan. I want your opinion of him, and then I want to tell you about the last two nights to get your opinion of some things. So, we all had dinner together the other night...what'd you think of him?" I leaned forward, propped my head on my hand, and waited for her review.

"As you know, I gave him two thumbs up. But to expand on that, because I know you're dying for details, I think he's great. He's got a good sense of humor. He's super attentive to you. He was watching you, like, the whole night. You know, in a good way, not a creepy, possessive way. He was polite, but easy going. He took the time to get to know me, your best friend, because he knew that was important to you. I didn't get any weird juju from him at all. So, yeah, you got my blessing, if you were looking for it. But more importantly, how do *you* feel about him?"

"Oh Bailey, he's better than any vague dream I had of what kind of man I wanted. He is so damn sweet. He's dropped everything to drive me around after my car got trashed. He's doing everything he can to keep me safe during this stalker thing. He even got his lifeguard buddies to keep an eye on me when he's at work. He called his parents for help, for God's sake! Wait...I don't know about that aspect though," I trailed off, lost in thought.

"What do you mean?" Bailey asked.

"Well, you saw his parents! They were dressed like they were going to a country club at 7 a.m. Hell, they may have been! They obviously come from money which makes me a little uncomfortable. They wanted me to hire a private investigator! Like they didn't even think money might be an issue. And then Ivan wanted to swoop in and pay for it. It just doesn't sit well with me.

I work hard for every dime I spend and I'm proud of what I've accomplished on my own," I explained.

Bailey reached over and grabbed my hands, stopping them from flying around as I spoke. "Esa, honey. Hold on a second. Remember, I'm on your side always, okay? But I think you may be overreacting to the parent situation."

"Wha-" I immediately objected.

"I know you've worked hard to do everything on your own, which is commendable. Truly. But just because someone has money, doesn't mean they can't understand your situation. You have a little bit of a chip on your shoulder about the money thing, Esa. I know why you do, I can see why you carry that chip, but let's not pretend it's not there." She was gripping my hands and speaking softly, delivering her blows with care.

"You've never mentioned this before," I argued.

"I know, honey, but I've seen it. What I won't do now is sit around and watch you carry that chip on your shoulder, using it as a weapon against Ivan, a man that seems really good for you. Could you at least see things from Ivan's parents' perspective? Here's their son, finally interested in a woman, after all the shit he's gone through. And this woman is in trouble. They have money, they can help her and therefore help their son be with the woman he's crazy about. Wouldn't you offer your money too? And as far as Ivan is concerned, the guy doesn't come across as rich and aloof. For the love of God, he drives a plain, four-year-old truck. He works out at a neighborhood gym, not a fancy, expensive boutique gym. He's not flashy or condescending at all."

I sat there with that, not speaking, just absorbing. I guess I did have a bit of an attitude when it came to wealthy parents wanting to throw money around. If I was being honest with myself, I was actually jealous. I didn't have parents to help me out anymore and that cut deep. I had to make things work financially as a very young adult, knowing I didn't have wealthy parents, or any type of parents, to bail me out if I messed things up. I was proud of what I'd accomplished but that didn't mean I should begrudge Ivan his parents' wealth. He didn't ask for them to be wealthy, it was just the situation he'd grown up with. And she was right, Ivan wasn't flashy at all. He was really laid back and, hell, he probably worked harder than me, even though he didn't need to.

Ah crap, I was overreacting, and I hated admitting it. I lifted my gaze up to meet Bailey's. She looked worried. Probably wondering if she'd pushed it too far. So I smiled and squeezed her hands back.

"I see what you're saying. And you're right. I was overreacting. I'll try to give his parents the benefit of the doubt from now on." I paused, then added, "Thank you for calling me on my shit, Bailey-girl. I think I was just picking a fight because this is all new territory for me."

That's when we hugged it out like besties do. And of course that led to Bailey asking if we'd slept together yet. I guess I did say I wanted girl talk.

"Well, not yet exactly," I replied with a secretive smile on my face.

"What the hell does that mean? Spill, woman!" Bailey leaned forward in her chair, ready for sexy story time.

I laughed at her eagerness and dished the details, knowing she hadn't heard any good stories from me in years. "Let's see, I guess we've made it to third base, if I have my bases right. Lots of making out, he's had me naked twice, and he's gone down on me once. Which, by the way, was freaking spectacular. The boy knows exactly what he's doing, which worries me a bit, but at the time, I was too caught up in his tongue and fingers to think about it. When I got my brain back to functioning, he wouldn't even hear of me returning the favor. He said he wants to wait until I'm ready. Said my ex must have been quite the ass to make me take a five-year break, so he wants to make sure I'm sure. And that's so crazy sweet, I can't help but trust him more, you know?" I rambled on as Bailey nodded her head. "Do you think I should be worried about my lack of experience compared to his? Don't you have to be, like, man-slut level to have that kind of tongue technique?"

Bailey burst out laughing. "I don't think you should worry about anything. Just be grateful he knows what he's doing, and he's doing it to you."

"Yeah, I suppose you're right. I know it's only been a few days, but you think it's okay to jump in bed with him?" I asked. I didn't understand the dating game, so I was super hopeful her answer was a definite 'yes'.

"Only you can answer that, Esa. If it feels right to you, then I say, go for it."

"I trust him. And I want to see if we can make this work. And I really want to see if other parts of him are as talented as his tongue." I giggled like a love-struck teenager. I couldn't help it. I was happy, I was having fun, and it felt fantastic to be light hearted. I couldn't recall the last time I felt this playful.

Bailey stood up, hugged me again, and said, "It's good to see you happy, honey. You totally deserve it. Now come on, we both gotta get ready for work."

Later that day at Chocolate Dreams, I got a call from Detective Ramirez saying he was emailing me a digitally improved picture of the man they got on the cameras at Pacific City the night my shop was vandalized. Unfortunately, the cameras from the underground parking lot surrounding my car were too blurry to produce any kind of image that would help identify the guy. He asked me to print the picture, study it, and see if any of his features looked familiar. I assured him I would. He also told me one other thing that sent my head spinning.

"Esa, I hate to say this, but it's my job to look at all angles.

Have you considered that it might be Ivan that's been doing these things?" Jack asked quietly.

My jaw dropped and my heart sank. Could it be Ivan? Could I be making yet another bad choice with men? I replayed all our conversations and interactions in my head, but it was too much to take in all at once. Jack must have figured my silence meant I was overwhelmed because he was quick to continue.

"Listen, I have absolutely no evidence it's Ivan, and I've heard only great things about him. But. All this stalker stuff started happening when you and Ivan started dating, right? If it's even remotely possible it's him, I want you with your eyes wide open, okay? Can you just keep an open mind and look for anything that seems odd?"

"Well sure, but Jack, I honestly just don't see this being Ivan. I'll think about it and let you know if anything seems weird, but I really think you're off base here," I explained.

"I hear you. Just think about it. In the meantime, I'll be busy over here seeing if we have evidence that leads to anyone else, okay?" Jack finished.

"Okay, that sounds good. Thank you," I responded. My mind was whirling, too stunned to focus on the conversation.

"Esa, I don't want to freak you out, but I want you to be aware. Are you sure you're alright? I can come to the shop and talk it through with you..." he offered. I wasn't sure if the offer was in the normal scope of police work or not, but it was sweet.

"No, I'm totally fine, Jack. It just caught me by surprise." It was just something else to worry about now. Could I have made another colossal mistake with Ivan? At the rate I was going, I'd be needing Botox at the ripe old age of twenty-six for this huge frown line that kept showing up on my face.

I hung up with Jack and placed a call to Strike Ready, the self-defense school downtown. I decided to just keep busy until I had some alone time at home to sort through everything Jack had stirred up. I spoke to a very nice lady who owned the school, and she explained how the classes run. She said Bailey and I could come in for a private lesson later this afternoon with one of her instructors. One-on-one time was helpful in the beginning, and especially given my stalker situation, she wanted to get a jump on my training. Bailey said she was available for the lesson at 5 p.m. so I booked it and checked that off my list of things to do.

Lastly, I got a call from my car insurance company saying they received the report from the police, along with pictures from the repair shop. They assured me that everything was covered, I would just need to pay the $250 deductible. That was good news, considering the repair work was well over $2,000. The repair shop assured them that my car would be back in my possession in just a few more days.

And then I attacked my shop with a bucket and a bottle of Windex. I gave it a cleaning it hadn't had since we opened. Some women eat when stressed. I clean.

Bailey picked me up at quarter to five and we made our way over to Strike Ready. It was a cute little brick building with several shops in a row. The parking gods were with us, meaning we found a spot within one block of the school. We both were in work clothes, which I'm sure wasn't ideal. But hey, if my stalker attacked, I couldn't very well ask him to wait till I put workout clothes on, so I figured at least we'd be keepin' it real. I decided not to share the conversation I had with Jack quite yet. I needed some time to process it first, then I'd hash it out with her.

As soon as we opened the door, a gorgeous brunette greeted us by walking over and introducing herself as Brinley. She was super tall and had muscles all over, highlighted by her tight Lululemon gear. Her hair was long and looked like it was high-lighted by the sun, rather than a fancy salon. She was literally so stunning, I just stared at her at first.

"So, ladies, how about a joke to break the ice?" Her voice was high-pitched and too damn cute. She seemed happy to see us, but also a little anxious and awkward. Which was weird because she was the gorgeous, fit girl of the trio, not us. Before we could answer her bizarre question, she launched into it. "What's the difference between Judo and Karate?"

Bailey and I looked at each other at a total loss for words. This chick was either hilarious or wacko, I wasn't willing to decide on which yet. We looked back to Brinley and shrugged to indicate our lack of an answer.

"Well, karate is an ancient form of self-defense, and Judo is what they make bagels out of!" Brinley finished her joke with a shy, expectant look on her face. She bit her lip and shifted uneasily on her feet.

There was a beat or two of awkward silence.

Then Bailey let out a loud cackle, doubling over as she laughed. "Holy shit, I almost didn't get it! Girl, you are straight up crazy. I like you."

I chuckled and watched Brinley's smile turn from awkward to warm.

She kept talking, telling us what we'd be doing in class that day, and soon enough I snapped out of my short-lived jealousy. This girl was clearly a nice human being, who happened to be gorgeous. You know those people that you instantly know you want to be friends with because they have a good, happy energy? That was how I felt about Brinley. There was definitely more to her than met the eye.

We were instructed to take off our shoes, so we placed those and our bags on the chairs lined up on the wall when you come through the front door. We joined Brinley on the mat in the middle of the room and warmed up with some quick drills. Then she showed us two moves: how to get out of a wrist grab and how to escape an attacker grabbing you by the neck.

Brinley explained how most attackers would be male, and therefore always bigger and stronger than us. So, we needed to think smart, using leverage and pain points to get away. We practiced each of the moves over and over. Bailey and I were so into it, we didn't realize our two hours were up until Brinley called us over to the chairs to chat. She said she was happy with our progress but stressed that repetition was imperative to reinforce what we learned. In a real situation, we'd be panicked and would need these moves to come automatically. We agreed to come to the group class once a week to continue our lessons.

We also exchanged cell numbers with Brinley, making promises to meet up at the beach some afternoon soon for some girl time. Brinley looked surprised at first that we wanted to see her on a social level, which made me wonder how many friends she had. Hmm...I could sense there was a story to this girl, but it was too soon to start digging.

Ivan may have his lifeguard buddies, but I decided right then and there to build a Beach Squad. It was time to surround myself with a whole group of kickass women. And I couldn't think of anyone who would fit the group better than Bailey and Brinley.

Bailey and I left the school, happy and sweaty. Having a stalker, come to find out, left you feeling out of control and wondering when the next attack would be. Taking self-defense lessons was a way to give me back a feeling of control over my life. I knew it was only one lesson, but I'd take any control I could get right about now.

13

*I*van had to pull some overtime the next few days so we spent at least an hour or two each day together whenever we could squeeze in the time, but we each slept at our own houses. Bailey was home in the evenings so I always had someone with me. She and I thoroughly went through the possibility of Ivan being my stalker and tossed that idea out the window rather quickly.

First of all, when my car got smashed, Ivan was here with me all night. It was highly doubtful that he snuck out of my bed, did his evil deed, and then climbed back into bed with me and I didn't wake for any of that. Secondly, I just could not wrap my brain around him being a bad guy. All the red flags I'd ignored when dating other guys in the past were nonexistent with Ivan. He was giving, caring, open, and sweet. Ultimately, I just decided that I was way smarter now and I could trust myself. There was no way I was misreading this thing with Ivan.

Bottom line: I trusted Ivan. Case closed.

Damn, it felt so good to trust myself. To trust my judgement about a man. I realized that the last six years since my parents died was about more than working toward my dreams, but also a way to get in touch with myself. To recalibrate and trust myself again. To know I'd come out the other end of an emotional roller-coaster stronger and wiser made me crazy happy and made me feel calm, even with a psycho after me.

Thankfully, no other stalker incidences had occurred this last week, which ironically, also irritated me. I almost hoped he'd try something so he would be identified and caught. Then I'd know the whole thing was over. Just waiting for him to attack was making me a little cranky. And quite frankly, it was putting a crimp in my plans with Ivan.

Bailey was meeting me at Chocolate Dreams this afternoon once she got off work. It was one of those early spring days that tricks you into thinking summer was here. No clouds, the sky was bright blue, the ocean was sparkling, and virtually no wind made for a postcard perfect Surf City day. Which means, the Beach Squad was hitting the beach! We were slammed at the shop all day, but I'd been working six days straight and there was no way Bailey was taking no for an answer when it came to getting out on the beach and soaking up some sun.

Earlier, I texted Brinley inviting her for a leisurely afternoon run with us which she was totally down for. I made sure she knew our fitness level, so she wasn't disappointed with our snail's pace. She laughed and said she'd treat it as some light activity to add to her day's workout routine. I'd have to question her about how she got that fit body. I was predicting it required giving up my daily hot chocolates which was an immediate no-go for me.

I'd just take a little extra cushion on my curves, thank you very much.

Bailey flew into the shop and pulled me away from the cash register. Jaz gave me a thumbs-up that she had everything handled and we crossed PCH, then walked down the strand toward the pier. We found Brinley at one of the volleyball nets chatting it up with a bunch of other players. She saw us, broke away from the group to trot toward us, and jumped to high five us. That was more enthusiasm than we'd ever showed for our beach runs before, but hey, I liked her energy. We left our flip-flops in a pile by the volleyball nets, went down by the water's edge, and began to jog heading south, away from the pier.

Right as we started our jog, I noticed a fully dressed man standing higher up on the sand, away from the water. He was dressed in all black; jeans, shirt, and baseball hat, which was odd for a day at the beach. I said between labored breaths, "Hey ladies...don't look now...but see that guy...in all black? Let's keep...an eye on him...okay?"

They both glanced around inconspicuously and spotted him.

"I'm proud of you, Esa. Being aware of your surroundings is the most important aspect of self-defense. Knowing who and what's going on around you is the best way to keep shit from happening. And he does look a little shady. We'll keep an eye out, don't worry," Brinley responded. I heard her, but was distracted thinking about how she was able to say all that without even pausing to catch her breath. I wasn't that out of shape, was I? I gotta say though, comparisons aside, I was feeling better and better about our developing friendship. This girl could kick some serious ass, and I for one, wanted to be around to watch that happen.

Bailey and I were both clearly trying to impress Brinley or maybe her athleticism was rubbing off on us already. We made it almost a whole mile before we had to slow to a walk and catch our breaths. We talked as our heart rates slowed down, finding out more about Brinley and what we all liked to do around HB. We turned around after we passed Beach Blvd, heading back toward the pier. I looked to my right and saw the man in black at the same time Brinley spotted him.

"Okay, girls, that's officially a little odd. Let's pick up the pace and head back to the pier where it's more populated. I'll keep watching behind us to see if he follows. Got it?" Brinley's sweet voice barked out orders, a clear sign she was as concerned as we were.

We nodded our understanding and brought our pace back up to a fast jog. We'd only gone about ten feet when Brinley said, "Shit, he's following us."

"What...the hell...do we do?" I gasped.

"See that lifeguard truck up ahead? We'll run to that and get the lifeguard to help us. Just gotta make it to the truck, okay?" Brinley encouraged.

We surged ahead and ran straight to the truck. I'd heard adrenalin could help in a fight-or-flight situation and I was happy to be prove that little factoid correct. I didn't think I'd ever run this fast on the treadmill at the gym. Maybe that would be the next hot fitness trend: hire a psycho to chase you till you either drop or burn off last night's cheeseburger. If the hot chocolate biz didn't last, maybe I'd explore that one.

The lifeguard exited the truck as he saw us approaching. I'm sure the sheer terror on our faces, along with three grown women sprinting toward him, gave us away as having an emergency. He was tall, good looking, and most importantly, he was a ripped, muscular guy. Forget life guard, he'd make a good body guard. Remember, it may be an emergency situation, but there's always time to appreciate a gorgeous male.

"There's a guy in all black following us," Brinley quickly informed him. Thank God she was here. Bailey and I were still just trying to catch our breaths without toppling over.

"I see him. Get in the truck, ladies. I'll call it in. Esa, right?" the lifeguard asked me. I nodded yes, and he continued. "If you have a phone on you, you better call Ivan. He'll want to know you're okay."

He then wasted no time ushering us into the truck before grabbing his radio and alerting someone at Headquarters about the situation. The man in black stopped running when he saw us in the truck. He continued to approach the truck at a cautious walk.

"Sir, I need you to stay away from the truck," the lifeguard ordered the man. Brinley watched avidly out the back window, probably waiting to see if she needed to jump into the fray at some point.

With his hands out to the side in a gesture of peace, the man stopped about twenty feet away and hollered back, "I'm supposed to be following Esa Grant. I've been hired to shadow her and apprehend her stalker. I have my private detective license in my back pocket. I'll get it and show you, okay?"

I whipped my head around and stared at him. What the hell was this?

I exited the truck to stand next to the life guard. "I didn't know I had a private detective on my case." I crossed my arms on my chest and squinted my eyes trying to get a good look at the guy's face.

"You stay here. I'll go check out his license and verify he is who he says he is. Meantime, call Ivan." He gave me a pointed look before walking away to deal with the man in black.

I whipped out my phone, saw five missed calls from Ivan, all from earlier today. I ignored the voicemails and called his cell phone. He answered on the first ring. "Esa? You okay?"

"I think so. Bailey, Brinley, and I are on the beach. We were being followed by this guy, so we got ahold of one of your life-guard buddies. But now the guy is saying he's my private detective. What the hell is he talking about?" I was starting to get a bad feeling about this. I mean, I had a bad feeling about this when I first spotted the guy at the beginning of our run, but now I had a different bad feeling.

"Yeah, that's what I was trying to call and tell you about this morning. My parents called me and said they went ahead and hired that detective last night. He's supposed to be shadowing you as of today," Ivan explained.

There was a long, silent pause as I digested what he said. I started to feel warm, like seeing a red haze, I was so warm. A weird buzzing noise filled my head and I couldn't process everything that was so very wrong with what he said.

"They WHAT?!" I yelled into the phone.

"Uh oh, that's not good. Esa, like, almost never yells at people," Bailey loud-whispered to Brinley from inside the truck.

"Okay, where are you?" Ivan demanded.

"Um, lifeguard tower nine. Why?" I was trying to take deep breaths. I was trying to push down the volcano of pissed-off that was trying to erupt from my mouth.

"Stay there. Do not leave. You hear me? I'll be there in ten." Then he hung up on me. I stared at my phone as if it held all the answers to my problems.

"Did he just hang up on ME? That's not how this works. I'm the one who's mad. If anyone gets to hang up, it's me. I'm calling him back..." I tried to redial Ivan's cell. Bailey jumped out of the truck and grabbed the phone out of my hands, which didn't help the volcano, let me tell you. If looks could kill, and all that.

"Esa, honey, I think you need to focus on more important things right now. First, we're safe. That guy is here to protect you, not hurt you. I'm guessing Ivan's parents went ahead with their plan, which is actually a really kind and sweet thing. They want to protect you too," Bailey said while holding my hands still.

"Yeah, but-" I interrupted.

"I know. They went about it all wrong. But taking it out on Ivan isn't going to help the situation. You need to calmly have a discussion with him and explain how you feel. You with me?"

I blew out a big breath. The red-hot, erupting volcano dissipated and left me with a smaller, simmering anger that burned in the pit of my stomach. I could deal with that. "Yeah, I'm with you."

The lifeguard came walking back over to the truck with the man in black. The lifeguard radioed in that the situation was resolved. The detective was in his early forties, had salt and pepper hair cut short, and a lean physique that displayed he was capable of his job. He thrust his hand out toward me with a grim smile on his face. I shook it reluctantly while he introduced himself as John Ruston, a private detective hired to help catch my stalker.

"My apologies for scaring you, ma'am. Mitch assured me they'd let you know this morning that I'd be tailing you," John said.

"Yeah, I was quite busy at work this morning and didn't have my phone on me, so I must have missed their calls." I couldn't keep all of my irritation out of my voice. The guy had scared me and I wasn't ready to let it go quite yet.

"My plan is to stay as far back as possible so we let the stalker do whatever he intends to do, but I'll be there to take him out before he does it. We want him caught which means making it look like you don't have protection. If you see me around, please don't make eye contact or otherwise acknowledge me. Here's my cell number," John said as he handed me his business card. "If you need me for anything, no matter what time, call me on that number."

"Okay, thanks. I'll be in touch," I responded. "By the way, your black jeans on the beach kinda gave you away. We do this fairy regularly so maybe a change of clothes would be good?" I couldn't quite control the snarkiness in my tone.

His left eye twitched, right before he gave a curt head nod and walked away, all business. I guess not acknowledging his existence began now. I supposed seriousness and focus is what you want in a private detective hired to protect you from a crazy person.

That was when I noticed Ivan walking, or rather stalking, his way toward me across the beach. Based on his body language and the scowl on his face, he looked angry. Again though, why was he pissed? I'm the one who should be pissed off. Clearly, I'd have to explain how arguments worked, because he had this all backward.

He did that chin lift "hello" thing to his lifeguard buddy once he reached our group, but never took his stormy eyes off me. Then he assumed the male power pose: feet planted wide apart, arms crossed over the puffed-up chest. So naturally, I assumed the female power pose: hip cocked out, hand on hip, head tilted to the side, look of bored challenge on my face. Too bad I didn't have any gum. Chewing loudly and popping bubbles would really complete my pose.

Never mind. Even without, this should be interesting.

Bailey came up next to me, ignoring the body language stand-off happening between Ivan and I. She explained she and Brinley would ride back in the truck to the volleyball nets. She'd wait for me there. Ivan finally took his gaze off me to tell Bailey she could take off. He'd be taking me home. She looked at me, I nodded in agreement, she handed me my cell phone back, and she took off.

"Are you okay?" Ivan asked softly, in direct opposition to his power pose.

What was this? I was all ready to argue, and he started with a gentle question? I didn't know what to do with that except answer it truthfully. "Yeah, I'm okay now. I was really freaked out earlier but I'm better now."

"Good. I'm sorry you were frightened. That's the last thing I want," Ivan continued in that soft voice. It's like he knew I was mad, which is why he was in that stance, but underneath all that defensiveness he cared about me.

I let out a big sigh, dropped my power stance, and just

grabbed his arms. This was stupid. Bailey was right. I didn't want to fight, I just wanted him to understand why I was upset. "Ivan, I specifically said no to the private detective. Your parents went behind my back and hired him anyway. I don't appreciate them going against my wishes like that. And I really don't appreciate being caught unaware, making a huge scene in front of my friends, and yours, and then ending up looking like a fool. Do you understand where I'm coming from?"

Ivan dropped his power stance too, grabbing my hands in his, pulling me closer to him. "I totally see what you mean. In my parents' defense, they were doing what they thought was necessary to protect you. They know I care about you, that you're special to me. I talked to them last night and told them about being questioned by Detective Ramirez."

"What? Why?" I asked, stunned that Jack had officially questioned him.

Ivan gave me a knowing stare and continued, his jaw tight with anger. "Apparently, he thinks your stalker could have been me, based on the timing of us dating. Did he share this with you?"

I knew I had to tread lightly here. Ivan needed to know I trusted him. "Yes, he shared it with me a while ago and I told him I'd think about it. And I did."

Ivan cocked his head to the side and gritted out, "And what did you decide?"

I moved closer, put my hands on his chest and looked him right in the eye. "I know there's no way this attacker could be you. I've made some bad judgement calls in my past, but I've learned from them. I absolutely do not believe you would do anything to hurt me. I trust you, Ivan."

After a long couple seconds of silence, his shoulders dropped, and he blinked. Then he nodded his head slowly. "Good. I'm glad you trust me. Because I would never hurt you, Esa. Ever. Hurting you would just hurt me. And I explained all this to my parents which is why they insisted on hiring that private detective. They want this bastard caught so you and I can be free to see where this relationship is going, without some psycho hanging over our heads." Then he leaned down and kissed me lightly. "Thank you for trusting me, baby," he whispered.

I smiled back and enjoyed his arms around me, holding me close. Crisis averted.

Ivan chuckled. "And I did try calling you like five times today to warn you about the detective, but you didn't check your phone."

"Why are you laughing?" I asked, pulling back. The volcano was starting to rumble again.

That just made him laugh harder. "Ya' gotta admit, it is pretty funny. You were running from the guy who was supposed to be protecting you! He probably didn't know what the hell was wrong with you."

"Ohh...that is not nice. There is nothing funny about this at all," I said, fighting the smile on my face, hands now on my hips.

Ivan calmed himself, gave me another quick kiss and then continued, placating and soothing me in a way that felt genuine. "It was a misunderstanding. An unfortunate one for sure, but it was no one's intention to make you feel like a fool. I'm sorry you felt that way." His arms wrapped around my waist once more and I couldn't hold on to any further anger. We both chuckled at how silly I must have looked.

"I know. I'll try to let that part go," I agreed. "But I'm still not happy with your parents for making this decision without consulting me. They can't just go throwing their money around like that. I'm not some charity case or a child they need to take care of. I'm perfectly capable of taking care of myself and making good decisions. I already feel like my life is out of control with this stalker out there waiting to pounce and wreak havoc. Your parents took away a little more of my control by taking this decision about the private detective away from me."

"I completely see what you're saying. I can see that having

some sort of control over your life is important right now. But I also know that sometimes we can't make the best decisions for ourselves because we're too involved in the situation. My parents saw that they could help, and they did. They aren't 'throwing their money around' or think of you as a charity case. They happen to have money and they want to use it for people they care about."

Ivan pulled me tighter, up into his chest. "Esa, you're the first girl I've been interested in since Megan. My mom's so over the moon excited that I'm finally dating someone, she already sees you as her daughter. And I know you've been without parents for a while now, but maybe you need a little reminder that parents would do anything for their children. Let them take care of you. Allow them that privilege."

My eyes started to tear up, and I was at a loss for words. It felt like someone was sitting on my chest, a feeling I hadn't had since the year following my parents' death. Had I judged this whole situation wrong? Were they just doing what parents do? Maybe I had forgotten the way parents are with their kids. Maybe it was time to admit I needed help and let them, and Ivan, be there for me. I wasn't sure how to do that, but I was guessing it meant I needed to just enjoy the fact that they hired the private detective and I was protected.

I'd spent six years now being the most independent woman I could be. Because I had to. Because there wasn't a safety net in the form of parents to bail me out in life. Survival meant doing everything myself, being responsible, figuring shit out on my own. Asking me to now let other people in would take a whole new set of skills. But I suppose if Ivan was taking a chance with his heart by letting me in, I needed to take a chance and let him into mine too.

As one tear escaped my eye and ran down my cheek, I looked up at Ivan and whispered, "Okay." He cupped my cheek with his hand, wiped my tear with his thumb, and pulled me in for a kiss.

It was sweet, it was tender, and it was full of promise. And as it always seemed to do, it got heated. Tongues battled, teeth nipped, and I wanted to climb my way up his body to get as close as possible.

"Let's take you home, baby," Ivan whispered as he pulled away from the kiss. I smiled and nodded, knowing we'd had our first argument and come out the other side in one piece. I'd said what needed to be said, he'd listened, and then we'd talked it out. I felt heard and respected, not brushed aside or ridiculed. And what a beautiful thing that was in a relationship.

14

*I*van walked me back to my flip-flops laying in the sand next to the volleyball nets. Then he took me home in his giant truck. We held hands the whole way, and he stroked the back of my hand with his thumb. He kept sneaking glances at me. Probably to make sure I wasn't reverting back to mad. Or that I wasn't revving up the crying bit.

"Don't worry, I've totally let it go," I assured him. "Your parents were trying to help and I appreciate it. It is kind of funny when I think about it now. I thought the private detective hired to protect me from an attack *was* my attacker! He probably thought I was crazy." I couldn't help but laugh again at what we must have looked like running away from him like crazy women. "One thing to know about me: I may get angry and tell you all about it, especially if you're my reason for being angry, but I don't hold onto it for long."

"Good to know. That just means after we fight I know we'll get to the make-up sex quickly," Ivan answered me with a sly grin.

"Ha! I suppose you're right, lucky boy," I said with a sultry smile. I squirmed in my seat as his hand traveled higher up my thigh. Speaking of make-up sex, I thought I was ready to take that next step with Ivan.

"Is Bailey home tonight?" he asked innocently.

Yeah right, I knew better than to think Ivan's brain hadn't gone to the same place mine had. "She said she had a date tonight, so she's probably at home getting ready right now. Wanna stay for dinner with me? I'm not the world's best cook, but I can grill us up some shrimp and make a salad. See? I eat healthy too!" I chuckled as I remembered the two hot chocolates I had earlier today to keep me going while the shop was hopping. I just wouldn't tell Ivan about that part...

"I'd love to stay for dinner. And that sounds fantastic. Can I get another taste of you for dessert?" He lifted my hand, still wrapped in his, up to his mouth to give it a sweet kiss.

I blushed as I remembered exactly what that mouth could do in other areas of my body. Ivan looked over at me, smirked, and continued to make out with my hand. His tongue darted out, and I had to press my thighs together to quell the instant desire. Then he sucked on my finger and I couldn't stop the soft moan from leaving my lips. That damn smirk came out again, right as he swung his truck into my driveway.

Ivan came around the truck to open my door and help me out. I didn't need help, but I wasn't going to waste a good opportunity to slide down his hot body as he helped me down. He walked me up to my house, looking around the neighborhood, being super attentive to someone potentially following me. I was just stepping onto my front door step to unlock the deadbolt, when a bright flood light came on. I looked up and saw that my porch light was not only working again, but it was like we were standing in the light of a thousand suns.

I looked over at Ivan who shrugged his shoulders. "I came by yesterday when you were working and changed out the bulb." Like it was no big deal. Like it wasn't the most thoughtful thing a boy had ever done for me. Something so little I needed, yet he made it a priority.

I left the keys in the door, dropped my bag at my feet, and flung myself at him. I jumped, wrapped my legs around his waist, and laid a big, wet, appreciative kiss on him. Thankfully, Ivan's a strong, athletic guy so my unexpected launch didn't knock him over. He just wrapped his arms around me and participated in the kiss. Next thing I knew, my back was pressed up against the front door, my front pressed into his hard body. Then the front door gave way, and we burst into the house. Ivan spun me around and pressed me into the wall, the door slammed shut, and the lock engaged. In all that maneuvering, Ivan's lips never left mine, his hips pressing into my body to keep me in place. The man had talent, what can I say?

"What the hell was that?" I said breathlessly when we came up for air.

"Babe, you have a stalker after you. We can't be making out on your front doorstep for everyone to see. I gotta keep you safe so I can make sure I keep getting these unexpected kisses from you. I'm kinda addicted to them. Addicted to you." I could feel how addicted he was to me and I couldn't help rubbing myself up and down his length, trying to satisfy the ache I felt there.

"That's good, because I'm kinda addicted to you too." I kissed him all over his face, just like he did that morning when he slept over the first time. "Some cute guy did that once, and I liked it." That earned me a genuine smile and an ass squeeze. Note to self: do that more often.

As much as I wanted to continue this foreplay, Bailey was still in the house. I made a silent promise to my happy place for future orgasms if she'd just wait another hour till we were alone.

I dropped my legs from around Ivan's waist, slid down his body again. "I gotta make dinner. Want to watch TV in the living room while I get the grill going?"

"Actually, I think I'll hop in the shower, if that's okay?" Ivan asked, adjusting the front of his jeans uncomfortably.

"Yeah, of course. Make yourself at home." My face heated, and I felt my lips pull up into a smirk knowing I caused that.

Ivan went up to my room to shower while I started dinner. I already had some bagged salad mix, so I threw that in a bowl and tossed the dressing. I was about to head out and put the shrimp on the grill when Bailey came through the kitchen. She had on a teeny tiny royal blue dress with cut-outs along the waist area giving glimpses of her smooth, flawless skin. She'd teased out her hair, accentuating her big, sassy curls. High heeled, sling back silver platform shoes completed the look.

I whistled my approval at her. She twirled around and then gave me a saucy pose. "I'm meeting that guy I met at work the other day, remember?" I nodded, and she continued, "He seemed like a successful guy, so we'll see if he's an asshole or not. I plan to be home around 11 p.m. If that changes, I'll text you okay?"

"All right girl, have a great time. You look fantastic. Make sure he treats you right, okay?"

"Will do. Have fun with Ivan tonight..." She winked at me, which of course, made me flush red again. I knew what she meant with that little wink. She laughed as she went out the front door.

"Get out of here, bitch!" I yelled after her, only making her laugh harder.

Dinner turned out great. I may not be an expert in the

kitchen, but I could grill with the best of them. Ivan kept his hands on at least one part of my body the entire time we ate, driving me crazy. We ended up eating quickly, both of us wanting dessert more than the main meal. Ivan did the dishes and cleaned the kitchen while I showered. I had to hand it to his mom, she clearly taught him right. Whoever makes dinner, the other one does the dishes. Isn't that like a federal law by now?

I was just coming out of the bathroom to get my pajamas when I spotted Ivan lounging on my bed, flipping through the TV channels. His eyes cut to me and they seemed to devour every inch of wet skin that wasn't covered by my towel. He dropped the remote on the bedside table, tracking me with his eyes. I walked slowly over to my dresser, putting a little extra sway into my hips. For the first time ever I felt safe enough to flaunt what I had, knowing Ivan was highly attracted to me in every way.

"What are you doing?" Ivan ground out in a low voice.

I looked over my shoulder at him. "I'm just getting my pajamas."

"You don't need them, baby," he answered smoothly. "Come over here."

I walked over to the side of the bed as he swung up into a seated position on the edge. He put both hands on my hips and pulled me directly in front of him, between his legs. He let both hands drift down my hips, over my thighs, and onto my knees where the towel ended. Then he reversed his travel, but under the towel this time, leaving goose bumps on my skin wherever he touched. He kneaded my thighs, glided over to cup my ass, then massaged my low back. Then his hands came back to the front of my body at the top of my thighs.

"Spread your legs, baby," he ordered softly.

I immediately stepped my feet wider, lifting my hands to rest on his shoulders. Then, with my towel still hiding his arms and hands, he ran a finger up and down my slit. I gasped at the intimate contact and dropped my head back, eyes closed.

"Look at me." Ivan stilled his fingers until I brought my head back up and looked into his eyes, foreheads almost touching. The contrast between his erotic touch and not being able to see anything was a total turn-on.

He moved his fingers again, spreading my damp arousal. Then one long finger was inside me, pumping in and out in a steady rhythm. His thumb circled right where I needed it with each stroke. His other hand reached up to cup my breast and strum across the tip.

I was on fire, my breath coming in gasps and my knees about to buckle. "Ivan," I got out in a shaky voice. I was so close. Just a few more seconds and I'd orgasm without him. And I wanted him with me. I was ready to take things further, I was certain. "I want you," I told him, hoping he'd understand what I meant.

"You got me."

"No. I mean I want you inside me this time. Please, Ivan?" I begged, too turned on to care if I sounded desperate.

"In a minute, baby. Let go for me first, okay?" He added a second finger and increased his pace. The feeling of being stretched ratcheted up my orgasm timeline.

A low moan was all I got out before my eyes squeezed shut and my body exploded. Lights burst behind my eyelids, my knees gave out, and my whole body was on fire while also shivering. Ivan wrapped an arm around my waist to hold me up, and kissed me, swallowing my moans. Next thing I knew, my towel was gone and Ivan flipped me to lay on my back on the bed.

As I came back down, I lay there catching my breath, my body completely limp and relaxed.

Ivan stood up at the side of the bed, looking down at me. He tilted his head and spoke quietly. "You sure?" He was giving me an out if I wanted it. I knew he'd give it to me too, but I was beyond sure. I was totally ready.

I didn't answer except to smile and wink at him twice. His face lit up in a big grin, recognizing our cheesy signal. He took his t-shirt off and all smiles vanished as the need flowed through us both. He eyed my flushed, naked body on the bed, the heat obvious in his eyes and in the set of his jaw. I could lay here all day and look at his delicious body. The muscles, the tan, his strong hands beginning to unbutton his jeans. Oh hell yes, it was about to get *good*. His signature smirk came out as he realized how avidly I was watching him. Hey, he could smirk all he wanted if he had the package to back it up, amiright?

The jeans slowly lowered down over his hips, past his thighs, then Ivan stepped out of them altogether. I knifed up to sit on the edge of the bed, stopping his hands before they took off his black Calvin Klein boxer briefs. I didn't want to merely be a spectator anymore, this called for active participation.

"Let me?" I asked sweetly, looking up at him through my lashes. His answering smile was all the permission I needed.

First, I leaned forward and ran my hands down his torso, enjoying the feel of soft skin over hard muscle. Then I grabbed around his waist to bring him up against me, my face at his stomach. I kissed around his belly button, then moved to the side to get my lips on those sex lines I'd been dreaming of.

"You know, that first time you spent the night, I saw these muscles and swore I'd get my mouth on them," I whispered reverently in between kisses. Ivan's hand came up to run his fingers through my hair, his breathing picking up as I used my lips and tongue to pay homage to his body. His skin was warm and smelled of my soap, layered over Ivan's signature smell. It was straight up intoxicating.

My hands dipped to the waist band of his Calvins, slowly pushing them down. Then I reached in and grabbed his erection, freeing it from its confines. Not all cock is created equal, but this one was absolute perfection. Beautiful, or maybe delicious, would be a better word for it. My mouth watered and my thighs clenched together. I wasn't sure what part of my body wanted him more.

As soon as my hand touched him, Ivan made a hissing noise. I wrenched my eyes away from the treasure in my hands and looked up at his face to find his eyes closed and his jaw clenched tight. Then his eyes opened and I swear they'd turned a deep, navy blue.

I moved my hand up and down, teasing the length of him. And then I went in for my first taste. I licked across the head, then wrapped my lips around him, only getting half a second to register the girth of him before Ivan lifted me off and scooted me back on the bed. I was about to pout, but any protest died on my lips when I saw Ivan crawl up on the bed over me.

"I'm not done with you yet. You can play with me later, I promise." He took a nipple in his mouth, giving it plenty of attention before traveling south, leaving a trail of kisses. He grabbed my knees and lifted them up and apart. "Keep 'em there," he ordered.

Then he dropped his head between my thighs, used his fingers to spread me open and unleashed his talented tongue. I clawed at the bed, grabbing the sheets by my hips to simply hold onto something. Fingers found their way inside me as his tongue kept up its assault. Before I was ready, another orgasm ripped through me, tearing a shriek from my throat. It was intense and bordered on pain, the delicious kind that makes you crave more.

Ivan climbed off me for a moment as I lay there, spent. Then he climbed back over me, rolling a condom on. "Are you sure? You can say no, you know that, right?" he asked me, intensely studying my face.

"I know. And there's nothing I want more than you inside me right...freaking...now." I wrapped my arms around him and pulled him into me. Two orgasms down and the need for him was still strong. I wanted him inside me, part of me. So, I kissed him, using my lips to show how much I wanted him. He kissed me back, letting his hands roam my body, squeezing, stroking, just feeling my skin.

We finally broke the kiss, he pushed up on his arms, and then guided himself to my entrance. He pushed in just an inch, giving me time to get used to him. It felt so good I lifted my hips to let more of him come inside. He thrust shallowly a few times, then thrust all the way in, stopping there and not moving. I felt full in the best way possible.

"You good?" Ivan bit out, scanning my face for any sign of discomfort.

"So good..." I groaned, pushing my hips up, ready for him to move. I felt full, stretched, the delicious thickness of him making me crazy.

He must have felt my need, or maybe he was just responding to his own need, because he thrust into me in earnest, one arm holding his weight up, the other hand on my breast, teasing my nipple. I wrapped my legs around his waist, giving him better access, as my hands roamed his chest, shoulders, and back. I wanted to get as close to him as I could, our intimate connection not even enough.

He dropped his head to claim my lips again, his tongue mimicking the rhythm of his thrusts. The feeling was building again, which I didn't even think was possible. Three orgasms in under an hour wasn't something I thought was possible outside of romance novels, for me or for anyone. But I desperately wanted to come with him inside me. If he could just hold out a bit longer. Ivan was thrusting into me faster and harder, and I was loving it. He reached his hand down between our bodies to find just the right spot to get me there faster.

"Oh God, Ivan...yes...right there...just a little more...harder, baby," I was talking but didn't know exactly what was coming out of my mouth. I just knew I was almost there.

"Come with me," he said, gritting his teeth. He thrust two more times, then I heard him grunt, his thrusts faltering as his body began to shake. His ragged breath next to my ear was like a dark secret he was sharing with only me. His orgasm triggered mine, just knowing I'd made this gorgeous man lose control. I tossed my head back, my back bowing up off the bed, my body milking the end of his release, my muscles down there twitching as I came down off my high.

His weight dropped down onto me as we both tried to catch our breaths. He rolled us over, me on top of him, our bodies still connected. I laid my head on his chest and closed my eyes. I was officially exhausted. I was hot and sweaty and I didn't care that our skin was stuck together as we both tried to cool off while still being on top of each other.

I was drifting in that space between awake and asleep when Ivan stroked my hair. "Esa, baby. Would you look at me?" he asked gently.

I stacked my hands on his chest, rested my chin on my hands and gazed at him, eyes half open. He scanned my face and then his transformed into a lazy smile. "Who would have thought..." he said, more to himself than me, while shaking his head slowly.

"What do you mean?" I asked, starting to wake up a bit. I thought that was the best sex ever, but maybe I got caught up in myself and it wasn't all that great for him?? I stiffened, attempting to pull away. Ivan must have felt my body tensing. He tightened the arm around my shoulders to keep me in place and lifted his head to kiss my forehead.

"Don't take that the wrong way. I just meant I never expected for you to be that wild. I fuckin' loved it," he confirmed as he trailed a hand down my backside, pressing his hips into me. I could have sworn I felt him getting hard inside me again.

"Wild?" I furrowed my brow and shook my head, not understanding where that comment came from.

"Yeah, you rushed me in there when I thought I better take my time, and then the dirty things coming out of that sweet mouth..." He chuckled as he shook his head again. "That was so crazy hot to hear."

I blushed. Dirty things? What the hell had I said? "Um, could you clue me in here? I was just enjoying myself in the moment so...I'm not sure what things I said," I asked hesitantly. I wanted to know, but I also didn't want to know. And why the hell were we talking about it?

"Don't you see? That makes it even better. You were loving what I was doing to you so much, you didn't think about the words you were saying. That's hot, baby."

Then he rolled us over, still connected to me and began to thrust real slow as he shared what I'd said. "So big...harder Ivan...I love your cock...don't stop." Ivan was smiling huge and looking mighty smug. I was still blushing, from him repeating my words, and from the fact that feeling was building again. And I was right, he definitely was hard again.

Ivan suddenly lost the teasing look and his eyes went hooded again. "Come on, baby. One more time. I wanna hear you again. Can you talk dirty for me?" Ivan asked as his thrusts picked up speed.

"I don't know...mmmm..." was about all I could reply with. All embarrassment magically left as the tingles spread.

Ivan pulled completely out, ripped off the used condom, grabbed another from his jeans pocket, rolled that one on, and then came back to me. He leaned down to kiss me, then grabbed my hips and flipped me over onto my stomach, lifting my hips so I was up on my knees. He stood right at the edge of the bed, pulled my hips back, and eased his way back in.

The angle was good. Damn good. I felt every inch of him as he slid all the way in. I didn't think I liked being man-handled, but this was before Ivan. I trusted him to take care of me, and damn, was he taking care of me right now.

He started thrusting, his hands on my hips, our flesh slapping, and our heavy breathing the only sound in the house. It was like our own private porn soundtrack playing in the background. I pressed back to meet his thrusts, and he rewarded me by reaching around with one hand and finding my clit. Then he trailed his other hand up my back to wrap my hair around his fist, pulling my head up and back.

"Ride me, baby," he said, voice gravely and low. I complied, keeping a fast rhythm by pushing back to meet him, loving the feeling of him everywhere on me.

I began to lose my rhythm as my orgasm punched through me. "Keep going," Ivan ordered, a bit of desperation in his voice now. I started talking again, who the hell knows what, trying to contain my orgasm while still thrusting back on him. Then his hold tightened on my hip and he thrust into me all the way, dropping his weight onto me, pinning me to the bed for a moment.

Then he released my hair, followed by massaging my scalp. He pulled out, discarded the condom, and came back to bed. I'd rolled over and scooted up to lay my head on my pillow. Ivan laid down, pressing the whole front length of his body to my front while we looked at each other.

"Even hotter than what comes out of your mouth is this look on your face right now, baby. You're gorgeous all the time, but right now...your hair a sexy mess, your eyes soft, your face happy, your cheeks flushed...you're the most beautiful woman I've ever seen."

There wasn't really any good response to that except to snuggle closer and kiss my man like I meant it. So, I did.

15

*I*van spent the night. No hanky-panky other than naked spooning, occurred the rest of the night. We may be young, but I can attest there is still a limit to the number of orgasms one could have in a twenty-four-hour period. Plus, Ivan said he didn't want to make things uncomfortable should Bailey overhear us. I told him she wouldn't mind, but he said he didn't want anyone else hearing the dirty things that came out of my mouth. Those were just for his ears only. I couldn't argue with that.

In the morning, Ivan woke me again with kisses all over my face, but this time, he added a hand at my breast, playing with my nipple. Being the floozy I've apparently become in the last two weeks, I tried to entice him into some morning action but he again refused me, saying he couldn't be giving it out all the time. I reminded him that if he was trying to play hard to get, he was supposed to have done that before we slept together, not after. He found me hilarious, but he still wouldn't put out for me.

The next two weeks passed in a blur. Work was crazy busy, which was awesome. Thank God I'd found Jaz when I first opened. She'd become my right-hand woman. I couldn't have kept up the pace without her. Ivan and I spent as much time together as we could. I usually spent the night at his place as he didn't have a roommate that might interfere with my latest obsession: sex with Ivan. The man had stamina, thank my lucky stars.

Bailey and I still went for our runs on the beach, along with our twice weekly self-defense classes with Brinley as lead instructor. With all the activity, I would have to up my hot chocolate consumption to at least two per day, with extra whip, to keep my curves.

I didn't have any contact from my stalker, which was weird, but a nice break too. I started to wonder if maybe he'd moved on. Detective Ramirez told me that stalkers rarely do that, but a girl could hope, right? I kept looking at the grainy security camera photo. He looked familiar in some way I couldn't put my finger on. I figured if I looked at it long enough I might recognize something about him if he ever got near me again.

True to his word, John, the private investigator, kept his distance but was always hovering when I left my house or left the shop. I didn't even want to think about how much Ivan and his parents were shelling out to pay for his services. I tried to ask Ivan once, and he asked me to let it go. Said talking about it would only stir up an argument, and it had already been decided, so what was the point. Begrudgingly, I agreed with him, so I dropped my questions. The potential for make-up sex almost made me pick a fight anyway, but since I was getting it on the regular, I was sated enough to be reasonable.

Tonight, Ivan and I were going out to dinner with his parents. Ivan wanted us to get to know each other better, and I wanted to thank them for hiring John, even if I disagreed with their methods. I'd never had a meet the parents dinner, so I was understandably nervous. This called for some serious fashion advice so I forced Bailey to take me on as pro bono side job.

She brought home two complete outfits from Nordstrom for me to choose from. One was a plain navy dress that came to my knees, paired with a white sweater overtop. Shoes were tall wedges with wide straps, alternating white and navy, making the whole thing look a touch nautical, and definitely classy. The second outfit was a little black dress, halter style that came to just above my knees. The shoes were a high spiky heel with some fringe. Topping off the look was a tailored faux leather jacket. Both outfits were kickass and fit me perfectly.

I threw caution, and my budget, to the wind by keeping both, deciding to wear the navy to dinner tonight, saving the LBD for a date with Ivan. I didn't want to look like I was trying too hard to win over the parents so I added a bunch of silver bangles to my arm and my big, silver locket around my neck that had been my mom's. My usual make-up, some soft waves in my long hair, and I was good to go.

Now if I could just get my nerves under control. I had already met them so I at least had that meeting under my belt, but that was a surprise visit and under urgent circumstances, so by my definition, this would be our first real "get to know you" dinner. We'd already identified that I was a little rusty dealing with parents and if I was being honest, I was conflicted. I badly wanted parents again. I wanted that unconditional love, that sense of "home" when you're around them, that sense of safety. But I also didn't want to be disloyal to my parents, whom I loved so deeply, even today. I would never, ever forget them, nor did I think a new set of parents could possibly replace them. And who said Ivan's parents even wanted to be a parental role model? Maybe they just wanted to know who their precious son was dating, but had no real interest in me as a person. See where my head was at??

Would it be wrong to swig a shot of vodka before dinner?

Ivan had gone to his place to change, then was swinging by to pick me up. He arrived right on time, let himself in with the key I'd given him a few days ago. What said trust more than a key to your place?

"Esa? You ready?" Ivan called up the stairs.

"Coming!" I responded. I spritzed on my perfume and then rushed downstairs, stopping a couple steps up from Ivan. I put my arms around his neck, leaned in, and gave him a slow kiss. He wrapped his arms around my waist and then slid his hands down to cup my ass. That would never get old.

"You look gorgeous..." Ivan said in-between kisses. "I think we can be a little late." Then he slid his hands up my dress and palmed each cheek, squeezing.

I broke off the kiss with an alarmed squeak. "Hell, no. I'll make the very best impression on your parents and that does not include us being late to dinner. Uhn uh. Nope. No way." I pushed back on his shoulders and kept a stern look on my face. "Hands to yourself for right now. I promise we can play later."

I'd never seen a grown man pout and pull off the look, but Ivan managed it. He also managed to block my way down the stairs until I'd sworn to allow him that playtime after dinner. Then his smile came back out, he grabbed my hand, and off we went to dinner with his parents.

When we arrived at the restaurant in Newport, his parents were already seated at a prime table right by the glass wall overlooking the beach. They both stood and gave me a hug before we all sat down again, with Susan directly across from me. Ivan reached for my hand and held it under the table. He gave me a reassuring squeeze. We made small talk, ordered our dinner and drinks, and then they got down to the grilling.

"So, Ivan tells me you're a businesswoman. Would you tell me about that?" Mitch asked me.

"Sure. I own and operate Chocolate Dreams in Huntington Beach. I opened in November last year and things have been going great. We're already operating at a profit and I haven't yet done any big promotional things to advertise. I have some plans for this summer, as I'm assuming the hot chocolate won't be as big a draw when it's ninety degrees outside," I explained, warming to the topic. I was nervous to talk business with a successful business man, but this was my jam. I loved my business and could talk about it for days.

"How'd you get into hot chocolate of all things?" Susan asked with a warm smile.

"Well, I've just always loved it since I was a kid. I'd make different kinds for my parents and friends growing up. My mom and I used to dream of opening our own shop when I was out of college. She'd man the cash register and stock everything. I'd make all the recipes and do all the marketing. Unfortunately, she didn't get to realize that dream, but I did," I ended softly.

Susan reached across the table and laid her hand on top of mine. "I'm sorry to hear about your parents, dear. They sound like wonderful people. I'm sure your mom is so proud of what you've accomplished."

I still couldn't talk about my parents without getting teary-eyed, especially when a mom-figure was telling me she's sure my mom was proud of me. I only wished I could hear my own mom say those words. I blinked back the tears and gave her a small smile. "Thank you."

Ivan leaned in, put his arm around me, and moved the

conversation along, sensing I could use a minute. "You should hear the guys at work rave about her hot chocolate. They keep volunteering to check in on her, which I hope is because they want her hot chocolate, not because they're trying to make a move on her." He frowned, and I chuckled, finding that ridiculous.

"We must swing by soon and try these famous hot chocolates. Might be just the thing to cater in for my next company-wide meeting. I strive to make my employees happy and it would introduce more people to your shop. Why don't I come by this week, try it out, and then we can discuss?" Mitch asked me.

"That would be great, Mr. Whittington." I knew I was pretty much only pulling people in from Huntington Beach. If I could get some word of mouth going in Newport that could really boost my traffic. This could be a huge opportunity for me!

"Please, it's Mitch. Mr. Whittington just sounds too stuffy. I know I'm old, but I try to maintain an image of still being cool," Mitch said with a smile. He looked so much like Ivan, just older and more ivy league. Ivan dressed nicely but still looked like a regular guy. Mitch had that look, like you just knew his outfit cost more than yours.

"Sorry. Mitch, I'd love the opportunity, but I don't want you to do me any special favors," I assured him.

"What's the point of owning your own business if you can't spend your money as you please? If you had a friend that was great at baking, and they wanted a place to sell their goods, wouldn't you offer up a selection at your shop? It's not special treatment. It's just good business to carry great products and work with good people. You're good people, Esa. I can already tell," Mitch continued with a head nod and warm smile.

I smiled back, my heart warming up and my nerves dissipating. "And I can tell you're good people too," I said looking between Susan and Mitch. "I appreciate you hiring the private detective to keep me safe. You didn't need to do that, but I appreciate it nonetheless." I paused and then decided to share a piece of me with them. "It's been a long time since I've had parents to look out for me, and you doing that means a lot to me. I don't take it lightly."

"We're happy to be there for you in any way you need us, Esa. You just have to ask. And we'll be there for you even when you don't ask..." Susan said, then followed with a chuckle. We all joined in and just like that, any tension or anger over their hiring of the detective was so long gone, I forgot it was ever an issue.

We continued getting to know each other through the main course and over a shared dessert. When it was time to go, neither Ivan or his parents would hear of me helping to pay the bill. So I simply smiled, said thank you, and swallowed my instinct to argue. See? I was learning to accept help. Progress, baby!

The four of us walked out of the restaurant together, saying goodbye to his parents when the valet brought their car around. As they drove off, we started walking across the parking lot, then down the sidewalk to Ivan's parked truck a block away from the restaurant. It was dark out, but there were street lamps every few yards. I was breathing easy for the first time in several hours, knowing our first dinner together had gone well.

We reached Ivan's truck, my feet grateful for the promise of taking my heels off in just a few seconds. Ivan opened my door, helped me up, then slid his hands up to my cheeks and held my face, looking into my eyes.

"You did great tonight, baby. I told you there was nothing to worry about and I hope you see now that my parents are already on your side. Even if they weren't, it wouldn't matter. You're it for me, understand?" Ivan said with a seriousness to his voice I hadn't heard before. I nodded my head, not trusting myself to speak. That certainly sounded like a forever type comment. Or leading up to the three little words. A future together. I didn't know what to say back so I just let his words wash over me.

A committed boyfriend AND a set of parents looking out for

me? It was exactly what I wanted, even when I didn't know it, when I was running away from every possible dating scenario.

Ivan dipped down to kiss me, ran his thumb across my bottom lip, then released my face. "I believe you promised me something after dinner..." He winked, causing me to smile and then moved to shut my door. As he was walking around in front of the truck to get to the driver's side, I saw a shadow jump out from the bushes on the sidewalk. It was a man, dressed all in black. Before I even registered what was happening, he had hit Ivan across the head and was tackling him from behind.

I screamed and jumped out of the truck. To do what, I don't know, but I knew I had to help my man. I left the truck door open and ran up behind the guy who was still standing and wrestling with Ivan. Ivan was trying to fight him off but I'm sure the blow to the head and being attacked from behind wasn't helping matters.

I didn't think about what to do, I just reached both hands up and grabbed his shoulders, wrenching him off of Ivan as hard as I could. Then I kicked out one of my heels to connect with the back of the man's knee. He yelped and went down on the pavement to one knee. Ivan whipped around and punched him in the face.

"Call 911!" Ivan yelled at me, still trying to keep the guy down, doling out punches and avoiding getting hit back in the process.

I ran back around the truck door, grabbed my handbag, dug out my purse, which isn't easy with shaky hands, let me tell you. Then I hit 911 and immediately told the operator we'd been assaulted and my boyfriend was still in a fight with this guy. She asked for our location, to which I could only remember the name of the restaurant, not the street we were on. She told me to stay on the phone with her until the police arrived.

Then the guy landed a punch in Ivan's face, making me gasp out loud. I know Ivan took the punch, but I swear I felt it on my face too. I couldn't just stand there and watch Ivan get hurt.

And that's right when I finally saw the bastard's face. For a brief second, his pale face tilted in my direction and the street-light was shining right on him.

The phone slipped from my hand, landing with a crash on the pavement. Ivan looked over at me to see what the hell happened and the guy took advantage of the opportunity. He jumped up and ran, disappearing down the dark street. Ivan was at my side before I realized it.

"Esa? What is it? Are you okay?" Ivan was grabbing my hands, trying to get my attention away from the spot where I last saw the guy running away.

Before I could even swing my stunned gaze over and focus on him, a squad car pulled up, siren and lights disturbing the night. The car slammed to a halt right by Ivan's truck. The officer exited the vehicle asking, "Are you two okay?"

"He just ran down the street. He's in all black, maybe a few inches shorter than me. White guy," Ivan told him. The officer called it in for another unit to patrol a few blocks to see if he was still on foot. It was then I looked over at Ivan, seeing a line of blood trickle down from his split lip.

"Ivan!" I gasped. "What the hell did he do to you?"

"I'm okay. Just a split lip, no biggie." He used his sleeve to wipe up the blood on his chin.

"Let me see it," I demanded. I grabbed his face with my hands and yanked him down to my level so I could check it out. It didn't look deep, so I doubted stitches were in order. But still. That motherfucker hit my man and made him bleed. I was pissed. The kind of pissed off that mutes all noise around you and focuses your thoughts to just one thing: revenge. Nobody hits my man and gets away with it. Enough was enough.

"I know who it was," I said quietly.

The officer had stepped over to us, probably to ask more questions, but he stilled at my statement.

"Tell Detective Ramirez I know who's stalking me now," I told the police officer.

"Babe, who?" Ivan interjected, anger seeping into his tone. Anger toward this bastard who was stalking me, anger toward the fool who would hurt me or anyone else.

"It's Rylan Elliot, my ex-boyfriend," I whispered. I was starting to shake all over now. The adrenaline was still circulating from the attack. I was so incredibly angry that Ivan was hurt by this asshole, and now I was also scared. Scared that the guy who made me feel so badly about myself in college was back. Scared that he'd mess things up for me with Ivan. What guy wanted to date a girl with a crazy ex who would physically assault you?

Ivan wrapped me up in his warm hug, giving me comfort, when he was the one who just got attacked. I should have been comforting him. He stroked my back, kissed my hair over and over, saying, "It's okay. Detective Ramirez will find him and arrest him. He won't hurt you again. Shh...I got you."

More police arrived, including Detective Ramirez. They asked us a bunch of questions, during which Ivan never let me out of his arms. An ambulance also arrived, and the paramedics insisted on looking at Ivan's injuries, if for nothing else, in order to document what Rylan did to him so we could press charges. They put a butterfly bandage on Ivan's lip, took a look at the back of his head where he had a slight lump. No signs of concussion, thank God.

Detective Ramirez shared his theory that Rylan was upset I was dating Ivan now, so he finally attacked him. Who knows how long Rylan had been stalking me, just never making contact. The incidents all started happening right after I started dating Ivan as if he'd become angry that I was with another man.

We were then free to go home. Ivan and I would have to come to the police station the next day to press formal charges and also to take out a restraining order against Rylan.

Back in Ivan's truck, we sat at the curb with the doors locked, in silence. Ivan had a look on his face I just couldn't place. He was angry, I got that. But something else going on there too that I couldn't put my finger on. It was making me nervous. He wasn't talking and a part of me wondered if he was starting to regret dating me. I mean, hello? He just got attacked!

Before I could figure out how to ask him if he was having second thoughts, he started the truck, put it in gear, and drove off. He called his parents, speaking through the Bluetooth.

"Ivan?" Mitch answered.

"Where the hell was your private detective tonight?" Ivan barked out.

"What do you mean? Did something happen? Are you alright?" Mitch asked in rapid succession.

"Yes, dad, Esa and I were attacked right by my truck, outside the restaurant. Where the hell was that asshole?" Ivan's voice was getting louder and louder. I kept silent and pressed into the door. Ivan noticed my tensing, reached over and grabbed my hand, pulling me back to my normal spot. I wasn't afraid of him, I just didn't want to get in the middle of a fight with his parents. I'd just met them for God's sake, I couldn't be in the middle of a family "discussion".

"Are you okay?" Mitch asked, concern evident in his voice.

"We're fine. I have a bump on my head and a split lip. But why wasn't the detective there? The guy got away!"

"We told him to take the night off seeing as we'd both be there with you two at dinner. I'm so sorry," Mitch said, obviously feeling badly that he'd given the guy time off on the worst night possible.

Ivan sighed, ran his hand through his hair and down his neck. "It's okay, dad. You couldn't possibly have known. Can you just call him and update him on what happened? Esa identified him. It's an ex-boyfriend from college, Rylan Elliot. We need to locate him ASAP."

"Sure, son. I'll call him right now. Is Esa there?" Mitch asked. Ivan glanced over at me and squeezed my hand.

"Yes, I'm here, Mitch," I answered quietly.

"I'm sorry, honey. I should have taken your safety more seriously. We'll find this guy and get him locked up so you're safe again. You'll be okay tonight?"

The poor guy sounded heartbroken. "I'll be fine. Ivan will stay with me. And you couldn't have known he was planning to attack tonight. Please don't be so hard on yourself. I'm just sorry that Ivan had to get caught up in all this." I wasn't able to look at Ivan yet.

"He's a tough boy, can look after himself. We just got to spend some time with you tonight, getting to know you. We can't lose you already, girl," Mitch said in a low, gruff voice. He paused, cleared his throat, and then his voice perked up. "Please be extra safe. I'll have John covering you as soon as you wake up tomorrow."

"Thanks, dad," Ivan said at the same time I said, "Thank you, Mitch." My heart warmed in my chest as I realized just how much Ivan's parents cared for me. It was a familiar feeling, I just hadn't felt it in so long, I forgot how comforting it was. Between the dwindling adrenaline, Mitch being so sweet, and not knowing how Ivan felt, I was on emotion overload.

We hung up right as we pulled into my driveway. Ivan gave my hand a squeeze and said, "Wait here while I come around the truck to get you out."

My heart rate picked up as I realized he'd be outside again, totally exposed to that psychopath attacking again if he was stupid enough to hang around my house. My eyes darted around the dark, looking for anything that might be suspicious. Ivan opened my door, helped me out, and kept me close while we got up to my doorstep. The bright flood lamps came on, and I'd never been so thankful for proper outdoor lighting. Ivan opened my door quickly, we stepped inside and locked the door.

I let out a nervous breath, turned to Ivan, and burst out crying.

16

*I*van scooped me up and carried me up to my bedroom.
     I kept crying and buried my face in his chest, my
hands over my face, trying to stifle my sobs. I hated crying. I cried
so much when my parents died I think I just ran out of tears at
some point. Or perhaps I was so profoundly sad at the time that
since then, nothing else could compare, and therefore tears
weren't warranted. Either way, I hated that I was crying, knowing
Jackass was messing with my life yet again, but I just couldn't
stop. I hated that I was still paying for the mistake I made in
college. I hated that my mess had somehow come into Ivan's life
now too.

Ivan laid me down on the quilt, took off my beautiful wedges, kissed the tops of my feet, stroked his hands up my calves, skimmed over my thighs and hips, reached around to my back, and unzipped my dress. Then he lifted me to a sitting position. He got my arms out of the sleeves, then laid me back down again, my body like a rag doll, so drained from sobbing. I was still trying to get myself under control when he inched the dress down my body and finally tossed it to the floor. Then he stood by the bed and removed his own clothes, down to his boxer briefs.

The bedcovers were pulled down, and he situated me back under them. He climbed in with me, rolled me so I was facing his front, his top arm wrapped around me. Then I felt him undo my bra clasp. And then those strong hands were stroking my back, rubbing away my tension. My sobs slowed to just sniffles and hiccups. Then my breathing started to even out completely.

The next thing I knew, I was waking up on my other side with the morning sun peeking through the blinds. My eyes felt puffy, but I felt refreshed and ready to take on the day. Ivan was asleep, pressed up against my back. His arm was wrapped around me, his hand cupping my breast. Something about seeing his tan fingers on my white skin was a huge turn-on. I wiggled my hips in deeper to his body, earning me a sleepy groan.

"Morning, baby. Feeling better?" Ivan said, a sleepy smile evident in his tone. The hand on my breast squeezed gently and his thumb found my nipple.

"Yes, I'm feeling much better now, thanks to you," I said, after a small intake of breath as he rubbed his hips into my backside and I felt just how awake he was. "You got work today?"

"Mm hmm...gotta be in at eight. You?" Ivan responded distractedly.

"I work every day, but Jaz is there to open, so whenever is fine." I was a little disappointed to hear he needed to go so early, but I knew he loved his job and so did I, so I understood.

"Probably got just enough time for a shower, then I gotta go. You wanna join me?" Ivan asked as his hand left my breast to travel south. The man was a good negotiator that's for sure. I was already in a state where I'd do just about anything for him to finish what he started.

"Hell yes. Morning glory should not be wasted," I said.

Ivan let out a quick bark of laughter. "Did you just call it 'morning glory'?" he asked with disbelief.

"Um...yeah? Do you prefer 'morning wood'? Or how about 'full salute'? Pocket Rocket??" I responded, feeling a little uncertain now.

I could feel Ivan's body shaking as he tried to control his laughter. I was feeling all embarrassed that maybe I got my guy slang all wrong, so I tried an evasive maneuver by rolling abruptly out of bed, running to the shower, and calling over my shoulder, "Get your ass in here, slowpoke!"

I may have been an emotional mess last night, but one thing could be said about me, I got over shit quick. 'Specially when there was a hottie lifeguard in my bed offering to shower with me. And not only was he incredibly hot, but he was downright sweet and took care of me during my emotional mess. A complete man package.

Ivan didn't disappoint. He got in my huge shower behind me, no trace of laughter to be found. He ran his hand up my spine spreading goose bumps across my skin, then gently pushed my upper body down. I grabbed the built-in step in the corner of my shower with both hands, my ass up in the air in invitation. Ivan accepted immediately, filling me with his long length, aided by the slippery, warm water. He grabbed my hips and set a fast pace, careful not to thrust too hard, lest my face meet the shower wall unexpectedly.

I was orgasming in just a few short minutes, followed quickly by Ivan. He eased out and helped me back up. Then he proceeded to wash my hair and soap me up. Of course, he thoroughly washed my breasts, several times, but just laughed when I pointed out his repetition.

I returned the favor when it was my turn to wash him. I was extra careful around the bump on the back of his head, and I gave his healing lip extra get-well kisses. Then I had him facing away from me, his hands up against the wall, propping himself up. I was gliding my hand up and down his cock, soapy water aiding my slick strokes. He wasn't as hard as he was a few minutes ago when we first got in the shower, but he was making a valiant effort. Eventually, he started to shake and he grabbed my hand to stop my stroking as I felt warmth flood my hand.

He whipped around and grabbed me by the waist, sitting me down on the step with my legs out wide. He slid my hips to the edge, went down on both knees, and dropped his head between my thighs. Between his fingers thrusting inside me and his tongue on my clit, I had no problem falling over the edge again, gripping Ivan's hair and breathing hard.

Suffice it to say, showering with Ivan took way longer than by myself, but I wasn't complaining. This could easily become my new morning routine. After we toweled off, he went to make us some eggs and oatmeal for breakfast while I did "girl stuff" in the bathroom to get ready for work. It was when I was almost done with my make-up, when I heard a knock on the front door. A few minutes later, Ivan called up to me, asking me to come downstairs.

He waited until I got to the front living room. Then with a smile on his face, he opened the blinds so I could see the front yard. And there she was. My car was finally returned to me. Brand new windows, taillights, and tires. I was happy to have her back, happy to have my freedom again to come and go as I please, without relying on other people for rides.

Ivan still insisted on following me in to work, then walking me to my shop. Then he took off to cover his own shift, but only after I promised not to leave the shop without someone with me.

17

I waltzed into the shop with a ridiculous smile on my face. Might as well hang a sign on me: *Enjoying regular sex with my hottie boyfriend.* I tried to bring it down a notch so I could get down to business and talk to Jaz about stepping up in the company.

Just as I walked in the door, Jaz and two of our regulars were in a huddle jumping up and down and looking at Jaz's phone. A few stragglers were trying to order their hot chocolate while staring at the crazed out girls.

"Hey! What's going on here?" I called out as I walked over to them.

They all swung their heads in my direction and Jaz's face lit up. She jumped toward me, holding her phone out like I was supposed to be able to see what the hell was on there. "Holy shit! Esa! Check this out!!" she squealed as she finally reached me.

I grabbed her phone to steady it enough so I could see what she was pointing at. She had Instagram pulled up to a picture of a stunningly beautiful woman holding a cup of Chocolate Dreams hot chocolate. As I pulled the screen closer, I saw that it was a picture of Shea Smith, one of the hottest pop singers at the moment. In fact, I think I was just listening to one of her songs on the drive in to the shop.

"When was she here?" I asked Jaz, still in a bit of a daze. I mean, come on. A famous pop star bought my hot chocolate. You know, the recipe I tested out in my mom's kitchen back when I was a teenager and this was all a hazy dream. Was this real life?

"Must have been last night when Matt was on duty." Jaz paused, still staring at her phone. "Esa. Did you read the caption??"

I lifted the phone back up and read the caption. "Holy shit. She loved the hot chocolate! And she linked to our account and told them where we're located?! That's incredible!"

"I know, right?" Then Jaz paused. "You didn't pay her, did you?" Jaz asked with a serious face.

"No! We're not making the kind of money that I could pay her for a shout-out. She just did that for free! Oh my God! That's awesome! Let's play her music in here on loop for the rest of eternity," I said, only half kidding. "You think I could blow that picture up into a wall mural over there?" I pointed to the opposite wall where a boring picture of a cup of hot chocolate hung. Jaz just gave me the side eye and continued talking so I was guessing that was a no.

"She posted it this morning, so let's see what kind of buzz we get from it. I'll repost it to our account too with some HB/New-port/Orange County hashtags. Esa, this could be huge," Jaz ended in almost a whisper as we both started envisioning a long line out the door.

"I better go see if anyone's applied for the open positions I posted the other day," I whispered back. "Oh, wait! I wanted to talk to you too. Can you come in my office for a second?"

I laid out my plan for Jaz and some new hires and she was totally on board. There was more screaming and jumping up and down as she hugged me. She swore she'd be the most kickass manager Pacific City had ever seen. She left to go maximize our social media exposure from the Shea Smith post. I sat in my office, a big smile plastered on my face.

Owning your own business is a ton of blood, sweat, and tears, but there are also moments like today, when it's all completely worth it. I had a growing business, my own house, and a hottie lifeguard boyfriend who took care of me when I was crying last night and then took care of me again, in a totally different way, in the shower this morning. Life was fucking good.

Right before I was set to leave the shop for the day, the door opened and Susan walked in. She was her typical rich-lady manicured self, but along with her bright smile, she had a wrapped packaged in her hands. She went to get in line but I went up to her for a hug and to get her order. My boyfriend's mother doesn't stand in line at my shop. What's the point of owning your own business if you couldn't do what you wanted? A wise man said that to me once. I had her take a seat and told her I'd be right over with her hot chocolate. She was trying a new variety today, and I wanted to make it for her myself.

Once we were seated at a little table tucked in the corner of the shop, she laid the wrapped package on the table. "Esa, honey. I know we didn't get off on the right foot when we first met. I know we went ahead with that private detective when you didn't want us to. And I know we've moved beyond that and there aren't any hard feelings, but still, I wanted to do something nice for you."

She moved the package across the table to my hands. "I know you and Ivan just started dating, but I see he's so happy with you. And I see why. You're intelligent, strong, sweet, funny, and an altogether good person. He's lucky to have you, and so are we."

She was going to make me cry. In my own damn shop.

I took a shaky breath and tried to swallow the lump in my throat that threatened to come out as tears. "Thank you, Susan. You didn't need to get me anything though."

"I know, sweetie. I wanted to. Go on, open it!"

I took the package in my hands and ripped off the paper. The noise of the shop faded into the background, my focus solely on the treasure before me. The lump in my throat swelled and broke through. Tears ran down my cheeks as my heart felt both light and sad at the same time. I blinked rapidly to try to contain the gush and willed myself not to break down entirely. Out-and-out sobbing in public would be embarrassing.

Staring up at me from a black and light pink frame was a picture of me and my mom in our kitchen when I was maybe ten years old. We've both got aprons on and we're holding a bowl of chocolate she's helping me pour into a mug. There's a poster laying on the counter with my handwriting in marker that says 'Hot Chocolate - $1'. I'm looking at the chocolate with a gleeful, childish smile. But my mom...she's looking at me, not the chocolate. And she's got this look of utter and complete blissful pride. The look that only a mom can give her beloved daughter.

I felt Susan's arm around me as she gave me a hug. "She'd be so proud of you, honey. And we are too. I hope you don't mind that I asked Ivan to find a good picture from your photo album."

I turned my tear streaked face up to hers and smiled. "It's perfect," I whispered.

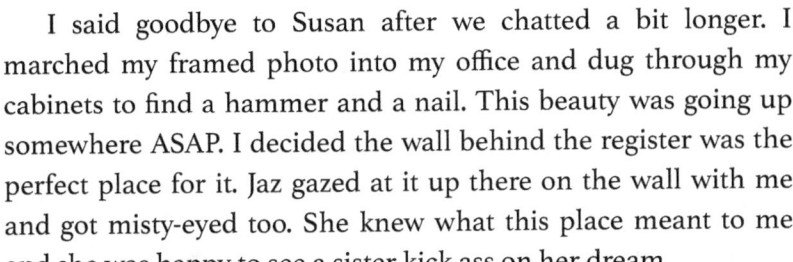

I said goodbye to Susan after we chatted a bit longer. I marched my framed photo into my office and dug through my cabinets to find a hammer and a nail. This beauty was going up somewhere ASAP. I decided the wall behind the register was the perfect place for it. Jaz gazed at it up there on the wall with me and got misty-eyed too. She knew what this place meant to me and she was happy to see a sister kick ass on her dream.

Then I attempted to leave the shop again, knowing my mascara had seen better days after all the waterworks, but got caught at the door by a tall woman in a professional, white pant suit. She introduced herself as a reporter for the OC Register. She saw Shea Smith's Instagram post from earlier today and wanted to interview me. Apparently, having a huge pop star rave about a local shop was the perfect reason to run an article highlighting a local business.

So, we sat down and discussed the history of the shop, how I got the idea, how I came up with the recipes, and my plans for the future. She wanted to angle the whole thing as a local girl turns business success story. She also asked if she could come back tomorrow with her photographer to get pictures of me, the shop, and even Ivan. Having a hot city lifeguard boyfriend made the story even sweeter, which I couldn't agree with more.

When I *finally* left the shop, I had Jaz drive me over to see Brinley at Strike Ready off Main Street. She was just finishing up a session so I sat in their waiting area chairs and watched the girls practice.

"They're doing so good, aren't they?" Brinley asked me as she sat down in the chair next to me.

"They really are. I was sitting here wondering if I'd had this type of training when I was a girl or even a teen, would I have avoided a few mistakes with men along the way? Would I have been more confident? Or recognized abuse for what it was?" I asked Brinley as I continued to watch these girls grapple with each other.

"Maybe. I'd like to think what we're teaching the girls here will serve them in the future in all their relationships. Even if it's just building their confidence enough for them to not get in situations where they feel uncomfortable. Have you met the owner yet? Shasta is her name. She's a firecracker. She went through some nasty relationship stuff and that's what spurred her to open this place. I'll introduce you next time she's here. I think you guys would have a great chat," Brinley offered.

"That would be great. In fact, I was wondering if we could put on a joint event. Maybe a self-defense seminar for girls. I'll cater the hot chocolate. Maybe we could get the Lifeguards to come in and talk about safety out on the beach and how to get help. We could donate a portion of the proceeds to a women's shelter here in HB." I was making it up as I went, but damn if it didn't sound like a great idea!

"Oh, Esa, that sounds great! I'll talk to Shasta and get you two connected as soon as possible. I'll donate my time to do the instructing and I bet I know a certain blond lifeguard who would donate his own time to help out with the event," she said with a knowing smile.

"I'll talk to him tonight, but yeah, I think I can convince him," I responded with a wink. Then I sobered and leaned in closer. "You know, with this whole stalker thing, it's lit a fire under my ass. I don't want to waste any more time in fear. I want to do everything I can to make my business and my relationships huge successes. And I want to make sure other young girls have confidence in themselves. I want them to have tools to protect themselves if, God forbid, they need them. In a way, I'm glad for all this recent crap with my stalker. It's woken me up. Does that make sense?"

"It totally does, girl." Brinley nodded slowly as though she knew exactly what I was talking about. "I'd say having a stalker would change anyone. And knowing you, you'll kick ass doing all the things you want to do. As part of the Beach Squad, the dynamic trio of HB female movers and shakers, I fully approve of this event!" Then we both laughed and hugged each other. We may only be three strong in the Squad, but the number didn't matter when the quality of the girls was so excellent.

"Okay. Off to build an empire," I said with a smile.

I left Strike Ready, looking behind me to spot John, my private detective, and headed down Main to hit up the Lifeguard Headquarters where Ivan should just about be wrapping things up. I probably should have just driven my car or had someone walk with me, but honestly, just getting out to walk by myself was pretty damn awesome. How much could really happen with John ten paces behind me?

I opened the door to Headquarters and several lifeguards were standing around talking, but they stopped and cheered for me when they saw who it was. My cheeks heated and I couldn't help the shy smile I gave in return.

"It's the chocolate girl!"

"Hey, we heard you're famous now...having celebrity sightings and all that."

"Damn, Ivan's a lucky guy...you let me know if you kick him to the curb, huh?"

"Haha, thanks guys," I responded sheepishly. I guess everyone checked social media a hell of a lot more than I did. I didn't particularly like the attention, but they were being sweet, so I guess I'd just take the compliment and find Ivan as soon as I could. I told my cheeks to calm down, but they didn't get the message. What could I say? These lifeguards were hot, and I was a warm-blooded female.

"Ivan told us you've been taking self-defense lessons. That's a smart idea. You never know what could happen and you want to be prepared to protect yourself," the tall, dark-haired lifeguard said. He looked familiar but I just couldn't place where I'd seen him before. He was good looking, but then again, that seemed to be a prerequisite to working here. While the other lifeguards were being rowdy, funny boys, this one was dead serious with his compliment and his facial expression showed he respected me.

"Thanks, that's what I was thinking too," I answered quietly.

"Esa. There you are! These guys bothering you?" Ivan said loudly as he entered the lobby from the back office. He came over to put his arm around me and pulled my body into his deliciously hot one. It was totally a possessive move, showing all his buddies I was his, but I really didn't mind it, seeing as how I was pressed up against a bunch of sexy muscle.

"Hi, baby," I said before I gave him a quick hello kiss. "No, they're not bothering me. But it sounds like you've been talking about me."

"Of course I've been talking about you. I'm crazy proud of you. I gotta brag about my woman," he said with a sweet smile.

And who was I to argue with that logic?

We turned to head back out the door, saying goodbye to the other guys. We'd almost reached Ivan's truck out in the parking lot when we heard a woman call out, "Ivan?"

We both spun around and I felt Ivan stiffen beside me. There was a small, middle aged woman standing a few cars away, shifting from foot to foot, begging him for something with her eyes.

"Martha?" he mumbled. He looked surprised and hesitant to approach her.

"Hello, Ivan. I'm sorry to interrupt but I was hoping to speak to you," she said quietly. She walked toward us, giving him a small smile that seemed marked by a permanent sadness. I didn't know who she was, but I felt the heavy tension so I wrapped my arm around Ivan's waist in support. He looked over at me and then when Martha was in front of us, introduced us. "Martha, this is my girlfriend, Esa. Esa, this is Martha. Megan's mom."

Ah, so now the tension made sense. From what Ivan told me a while ago, he hadn't had any contact with Megan's parents since he left for college. What would she want with him all these years later?

"It's nice to meet you, Esa," she said to me with a kind smile.

"Same to you, Martha."

She turned her gaze to Ivan. "I ran into your mother the other day at the grocery store. I just felt like I needed to see you, make sure you were okay." She rushed on, "I-I know we didn't speak much after Megan died. We were all grieving and I didn't trust myself to say the right things. But I've had a lot of time to think about everything that happened, and I just hope you know that Megan's dad and I don't hold any hard feelings toward you. You were not to blame for what happened that night, Ivan." She was still wringing her hands but her words were firm.

Ivan broke eye contact and looked down at the ground, his jaw clenching as he started to shake his head.

"Ivan. I talked to your mom. She told me how you felt afterwards. Enough is enough. You cannot keep carrying the guilt for what happened with Megan," Martha said more firmly while reaching out to touch Ivan gently on the arm. "She was our wild child. Always getting in trouble. Always dancing a fine line with danger. Yes, it was heartbreaking when she drowned, but we always wondered if she'd get herself in serious trouble. At least she went out doing all the wild things she loved to do. It was a freak accident and you played no part. Let it go, son."

Ivan's head jerked up and he met Martha's gaze once more, tears making his eyes shine bright. He nodded his head and then pulled her in for one of his famous hugs. They held each other for a long while, Martha crying softly and Ivan trying to keep it together. Then he whispered in her ear, "Thank you."

And that's when I realized that I was crying again too, watching them have their moment. These damn moms today were killer on my mascara.

I was happy for Ivan that he finally got 'permission' from Megan's parents to stop feeling guilty. I hoped that this would be what he needed to let that guilt go. He was a fine lifeguard and he could continue to do that without this heavy weight on his heart. In fact, I knew he'd be better at everything he did. The compulsion to always prove himself had only held him back.

We eventually said goodbye to Martha and got in his truck. We said nothing, the peace we both felt in that moment saying everything. We gazed out the front windshield, watching the sun set over the ocean for a long while, just holding hands and letting the day soak in. Then he started up the truck and we headed home.

18

*T*he next day, Detective Ramirez called my cell mid-morning to let me know, because of my positive ID from our attack the other night at the restaurant, they'd gotten a warrant to enter Rylan's apartment in Westminster, a few miles from HB. He was headed there now and would let me know if they found him.

I filled Jaz in on everything that was happening. She promised to keep an eye out and to make sure I didn't leave the shop unattended. She suggested I even go home, but I knew that wouldn't be a good option for me. I needed to have something to focus on.

Besides, Mitch and Susan came in a little later to try out my hot chocolate. I introduced Mitch to Jaz, we chatted for a bit, then I made them personalized hot chocolates based on their dessert preferences. I knew I had 'em when they both closed their eyes for a second after taking the first sip. Mitch had a big grin on his face when he set his cup down and declared it 'the best damn hot chocolate' he'd ever had.

"I've got a big meeting in about two weeks. Can we set up a hot chocolate station with maybe two or three varieties for them to choose from?" Mitch asked me.

"I can do better than that. I'll bring over one of my employees with me to man the station and create the hot chocolate from scratch right there. That way your people can order whatever flavor they want and they get to see the process of making it," I answered, beaming at the chance to introduce my chocolate to a whole new geographical area.

"Done! I'll have my assistant send you the details and we can discuss how much you'll charge," Mitch said before finishing his cup. Susan was still sipping hers and watching the long line of people at the counter.

"I don't know, Esa. You might need some more help at the counter. Is it this busy all the time?" Susan asked me, a worried frown marring her attractive features.

"Pretty much, yeah. I've been working non-stop, not only at the counter, but also the business aspect of it all. I think you may be right; it's time to hire more help," I answered with a nod.

The Whittingtons left soon after with the promise to be back next week some time for more hot chocolate. I got busy helping Jaz, and the day sped by. Jaz left at four o'clock when my evening employee showed up. In our shop bathroom, I changed my slacks and blouse for workout clothes. I was planning to head over to Strike Ready to train with Bailey and Brinley. My Lululemon capri pants, topped with a Reebok sports bra and racerback tank from Target felt super comfortable and I liked knowing I represented all economic levels of athleisure wear. HB may be getting higher end with their shops and housing prices, but I didn't want to go full-on Newport snobby either. Girl had to represent old-school HB too.

Fashion choices made, I called Detective Ramirez from my tiny office in the back before I left the shop. My call went straight to voicemail. I thought he'd have called me by now with an update on the search warrant. I was anxious to know if Rylan had been arrested yet. My safety, and that of those I cared about, depended on that info. We were so close to this whole stalker thing being over with and I was feeling impatient.

Bailey busted open the door to my office and snapped, "Let's go kick some ass, woman!"

My escort had arrived. I jumped up, grabbed my bag, and linked arms with her. We exited the store after saying goodbye to my employee, and we headed down to the parking garage via the escalator. We were walking down a row of cars on the first under-ground floor of the dim garage when shit hit the fan.

Everything began to move in slow motion like a cartoon gone wrong. A man jumped out from behind a van, grabbed me around my waist, and dragged me away from Bailey and back against his body. Bailey screamed, and I was completely frozen, eyes wide with terror. His free arm went around my neck and I felt something sharp jabbing me at the side of my neck. "Back away now or I swear I'll hurt her," I heard him say to Bailey. His voice was familiar, and it was definitely Rylan. I remembered his voice clearly and just hearing it made my whole body start to shake.

Bailey's face was a mask of fear. She had her hands out, palms up to show him she wasn't doing anything. She didn't move back like he asked, but she didn't move forward either.

Our movements may have been in slow motion, but my thoughts were on hyper speed. I was breathing heavy, and I was starting to get pissed, the anger matching my fear. I wouldn't let him hurt me again. I had vowed in college to be done with him and how he made me feel. And here he was trying to mess with my life yet again. Unacceptable! So, I had to stop him, plain and simple. I had to stop him before he tried to take me anywhere, I knew that much from what Brinley had taught me. And it was up to me, only me. Time for me to do what I'd been practicing: take care of myself.

With that thought, I sprang into action like my life depended on it, which I believed it totally did. I lifted my foot and stomped it as hard as I could onto his. At the same time, I used my trapped arm to strike backward in the region of his groin. My free hand came up and grabbed the hand at my neck. The foot stomp and the body jab startled him but I'm sure it didn't do much. But my other hand was able to get ahold of one of his fingers that held what felt like a knife. So, I bent that fucker back with everything I had.

Rylan yelled and let me go around the waist. I pivoted out of the way so I was facing him, still trying to keep his finger bent back. That's when Bailey jumped into the fray to help. She kicked him right in the groin and then kneed him in the face when his knees buckled. The hand holding the knife released, and it clattered to the ground.

I was just about to start kicking him as he lay on the ground when I felt arms pull me back. I struggled to pull free and got in one wild swing when I heard, "Esa, it's me," spoken right in my ear. I looked down at the arm around my waist and saw it was familiar.

Ivan.

I immediately quit struggling, relief zinging through my system. Ivan whipped me around behind him, putting himself between Rylan and I. I looked around him to see that John, my private detective, had moved Bailey out of the way also and Detective Ramirez was forcing Rylan flat on the ground, yanking one arm behind his back. Bailey came over and grabbed me in a bear hug, both of us wide-eyed and shaky.

Rylan was hauled to his feet, his hands cuffed behind his back. He looked right at me the whole time Detective Ramirez was walking him to his squad car parked halfway down the parking garage. He had grown older, disproportionally to the years it had been since I'd last seen him. His silent face showed a bizarre mixture of love and hate, twisting his features into something ugly. A look I'd probably never forget.

Ivan then joined the group hug, blocking Rylan from my site, doing more to calm me than all the hot chocolates in the world.

More cops joined us in the garage and we all gave our statements yet again. I was feeling like a pro at answering questions for cops and telling my side of the story. People were milling around, obviously wondering what the hell had happened. I felt super conspicuous and wondered, not for the first time, how I'd gotten into this predicament. You don't ask for a stalker, you don't do anything to make someone obsessed, but somehow you can still get drawn into this mess and you have to see it through. Hopefully this was my one life lesson on that and I'd never have to experience this again.

When they were all done, and they had the garage camera video tapes to back our story, we all decided to go home. The adrenaline had clearly left my body, leaving me with only exhaustion. I'd been here before all too recently and I knew I needed to get home. Ivan piled Bailey and I in his truck and he took us to my place, calling in a delivery pizza order on the way. Brinley had texted us multiple times, wondering where we were, so I texted her back and let her know we were okay but wouldn't be showing up for our class time.

My hands were still shaking, so I clasped them together and tucked them under my legs. I stared out the window as my hometown zoomed by, the sun about to set on one crazy-ass day.

"You know what they say about yoga pants, right?" I asked my truck-mates out of the blue. Ivan and Bailey looked at me like I was whacko, which was a fair assessment at that point. "They say you can kick ass in them because you have full range of motion. I think we proved that theory correct, honey," I finished, looking at Bailey. She and Ivan chuckled, dubbing my Lulu's my new "kick ass pants".

"Well, I am a personal shopper, you know. I like to think I keep myself and my bestie decked out in fashion appropriate gear at all times. We have a special 'kick your stalker's ass' line. It's disturbingly popular," Bailey added to my crazy talk. She and I laughed again, and I wondered if this would even be funny the next day, but right now, the level of tired I was, it was freaking hilarious. It was either laugh or cry and I cried last night. I wasn't due.

"You killed two balls with one kick, Bailey." I was full out laughing now, Bailey right there with me like besties do.

"And that's not even one of your jacked-up phrases!" she managed to get out. Tears were starting to leak out of our eyes we were laughing so hard. We kept swiping our eyes, our faces turning red. "Wait, wait. Get this. He brought the wrong utensil. He really 'forked' up!" Our laughter was almost silent now, with the occasional high pitched squeak.

"He really added assault to injury," I wheezed out. We doubled over at that one and I don't even want to know what we sounded like by now.

Ivan was shaking his head at our ridiculousness. "Freakin' attacked with a knife tonight and now it's word play time..." he muttered.

Boys don't get it. When we're tired, us girlies sometimes get the giggles. It happens.

We eventually calmed down and Bailey pulled me into her with an arm around my shoulders. "Life just ain't boring with you around, girl."

"Glad to provide entertainment for ya'." I smiled, then my face got serious as I looked at her. "And thanks for having my back out there. We totally channeled our inner Brinley. My Girl Squad is fierce."

"We've always made a good team. And always will," she responded with a squeeze, looking away before I caught her eyes getting shiny. She was tough, but my best friend was also marshmallow soft in the center.

"All right, let's break up this lovefest and get some rest, huh?" Ivan swung the truck into the driveway. We all let out a long breath as we realized we didn't need to be afraid to walk outside at night anymore.

My stalker was behind bars.

I was safe.

19

he next day, we decided to sleep in and take the day off work. I figured we had some resting and some celebrating to do. My plans for rest were foiled when my phone rang repeatedly as friends and employees got wind of what happened. Ivan, Bailey, and I ended up just going in to Chocolate Dreams and having an unofficial powwow there. Better to have this conversation once rather than relaying everything back and forth with dozens of phone calls.

Jaz and two other employees were running the shop while eavesdropping on our conversation. Susan and Mitch came in with John, who wanted to fill me in on everything that happened yesterday with the search warrant. Detective Ramirez swung by to see how I was doing, which made Bailey happy, I noticed. I think she was mesmerized by the dimple.

Brinley left the beach in the middle of her volleyball practice, which was almost unprecedented so I felt quite special. She insisted on a blow by blow account of the whole thing which I felt was her due, considering she taught us everything we did to thwart my attacker. And finally, some of my regulars came in and joined the huddle of chairs, wanting to know what happened and that I was okay.

Everybody had a seat or stood behind chairs and I was about to launch into my story when I had to just take a moment to look around at the group assembled before me. Ivan was right next to me, his hand on my thigh, giving support. Everyone else was clustered in around me, their faces turned to me, eager to hear how I was. I'd felt lonely for many years, adrift without a family to anchor me. I'd just put my head down and focused on building my life again. Graduating college, starting my business. Becoming an adult. And without even realizing it, I'd also built a new family, the ones sitting before me. A family that didn't have my past history to share, but one where I knew we'd have a long future to share.

Which was just as sweet.

It was with that warmth flooding me, making my voice strong and sure, that I got started on my story. I began with Bailey and I leaving the shop to go downstairs. When I got to the part about Rylan attacking us, I slowed down and really tried to remember everything exactly as it happened. It was a weird blend of that slow motion and fast forward that made it hard to recall correctly. But looking at Brinley, I knew she would appreciate the part she played in giving me the tools I needed to defend myself. She was nodding along with my story, a look of pride filling her face when I explained I couldn't let him leave the garage with me.

When I got to the part where Ivan, John, and Detective Ramirez joined us, I looked over to all three of the men and gave them the floor. I still didn't know why or how they showed up when they did. And now that I thought about it, why did they all show up at the same time?

Detective Ramirez, Jack, started speaking first. "As you know, Esa, we got a search warrant to enter Rylan's apartment. When we went in, he wasn't there, but we found plenty of evidence to prove he was the one behind the vandalism and stalking. I think you'd appreciate the truth, so I'll lay it out for you straight." He paused and looked at me with such a serious face, I knew I wasn't going to like what he was about to say. I nodded to him anyway, giving permission to continue. Ivan grabbed my hand and pulled it into his lap, letting me know he was there for me.

"We found a whole wall covered in pictures of you. From what we can tell, he's been following you for about a year now. There are pictures of you checking out this shop space before you'd opened for business. Pictures of you and Bailey outside your house, at the beach, out at restaurants. His computer had his email pulled up, and we found the confirmation for the lingerie he ordered online and then delivered to your doorstep." Jack took a deep breath and let me soak that all in.

His obsession made my stomach clench, but knowing he was arrested kept it from turning into fear. "I knew years ago that he was abusive, but to know he was that disturbed is scary. I thought after I got that restraining order on him back in college that would be it. I never did hear from him again, so I just assumed he'd moved on. What would make him come back years later and track me down?" I asked, not sure I would ever really get an answer to that.

"Another piece of evidence we found was a note written to you on his desk. It was basically a final letter in case anything happened to him. He said he tried but couldn't live without you. And he wouldn't sit around watching you move on with someone else. Esa, he was delusional. You may never understand why he did what he did, because it just doesn't make sense to those of us who don't think like that," Jack finished.

John picked up the story and all our eyes moved over to him. "Jack called me and I told him you were at your shop but getting ready to head out with Bailey. He said he was coming over to share his discovery in person with you. I then called Ivan and asked him to come over. I figured you'd want him with you when you heard about it. I waited outside the shop, looking for Rylan, wondering where and when he'd make his move. Based on the letter, I assumed he'd be coming for you soon to grab you. While scanning the crowd for him, I saw you and Bailey bookin' it down the escalators. I ran after you and met up with Jack and Ivan at the end of the garage. We heard your scream and took off running."

The storytelling ended, and we all sat there absorbing everything. Ivan reached over and brought me in for a kiss on my head. An overwhelming sense of gratitude swarmed me, making my eyes feel hot. I was surrounded by people who cared about me. I would be okay.

Bailey, being larger-than-life Bailey, couldn't handle the silence and stood. She lifted her hot chocolate cup and with a big smile said, "To my best friend who makes hot chocolate all of Huntington Beach has become addicted to. YOU, Esa girl, are as sweet as your chocolate and just as addicting. And Brinley, thank you for equipping us with what we needed to not only survive, but kick that fucker's ass. Cheers, Beach Squad!"

Everyone laughed and called out their own cheers while toasting us girls. Then I gave hugs all around, thanking everyone for making sure I was okay.

The group was beginning to take off when the reporter from the other day called out, "Esa! Back in the news, I see." She chuckled while giving me a hug. She'd heard about what happened and wanted to get the latest scoop. So one more time I went over the details while she took notes.

She assured me they'd run the new article in tomorrow's paper. I guess I would get my fifteen minutes of fame whether I wanted it or not. I'd always hoped it would be for something a little more amazing, but I guess escaping a psychopath was pretty good too.

Later that night, Ivan and Bailey got a bunch of food delivered just in time for Mitch and Susan to join us for dinner. They brought champagne to celebrate, and I got to give them the official house tour. Last time they came over I was so shocked to see them, I didn't get around to being a good host. This time around, I enjoyed their visit, getting to know them even more. They showed interest in my humble home and even wanted to look through old photo albums with me. I introduced them to my parents via old pictures and they asked me all kinds of questions, genuinely wanting to get to know them. It had been awhile since I'd been able to reminisce about them and about my childhood. It made my heart hurt, but it also felt cleansing.

I noticed that Ivan didn't let me out of touching distance all night. He either held my hand, had his arm around me, or just had part of his body touching mine. He wasn't smiling like usual and was overly quiet. It had been a crazy few days, and we hadn't really had much time to talk, just us. It didn't seem like he was mad at me, but something was definitely off. While his parents were checking out the backyard with Bailey, I cornered him in the kitchen.

"Okay, what's going on? You all right?" I asked, concern lacing my voice.

He wrapped his arms around me, pulling me in close, and I tilted my head back to look in his clouded eyes. He sighed and gave in to the conversation. "I'm fine. You just scared the crap out of me. To think that bastard could have hurt you and I wasn't there to protect you...well, it kind of kills me. You know my history. It felt like it was repeating itself. I know how strong you are and I saw firsthand how you handled the situation like a freaking badass, but I still can't help but hear your scream replay in my head. I don't think I've ever been that scared in my life. With Megan, it was shocking, and it was awful, but if something had happened to you..." he broke off and clenched his jaw.

My hottie lifeguard was worried. Over me. I squeezed my arms around him tighter and assured him, "I'm okay, babe. I'm sorry I scared you and I'm sorry it took you back to that memory. But I also knew in that moment, in that garage, that I could take care of myself. For all the times I've doubted myself because I allowed Rylan to cut me down, I've proven the opposite to myself now. I can't tell you how good it feels to truly know I've got my own back. Facing him and fighting back was exactly what I needed to put that part of my past away. So, you've got to let go of that scared, helpless feeling. I needed to do it myself." My eyes were begging him to understand. "I didn't want to be that girl that needs a knight in white armor to come riding in and save me."

His eyes cleared and his lips lifted on one side. I could swear he looked like he was trying not to laugh. "Knight in white armor? Babe." Then he began to laugh out loud. I didn't quite like that he was laughing at my metaphor, but knowing he'd dropped the scared and was embracing the lightheartedness I loved about him, was worth it. "Let's go outside, round up my parents, and get them out of here. I got something I want to show you in your bedroom," he finished with a flirty smile.

"Yeah, I bet you got something to show me..." I said, rolling my eyes. I acted like I didn't want to, but I totally wanted to see.

Ivan was above me, pumping his hips, driving me crazy with a slow, sensuous rhythm. He alternated between staring into my eyes and leaning down to kiss me when our breathing allowed for it. The moonlight was shining in through the half-closed shades, highlighting the dips and curves of his muscles above me. The ceiling fan was on low, making the sheen of sweat on our skin turn cool. At first I thought Ivan was being quiet and subdued because Bailey was in her room down the hall. But then the intensity of his eyes and the way he was prolonging our time connected so intimately made me think this was just his way of celebrating the fact that I wasn't hurt.

The pressure was building, so I brought my knees up higher and hugged them around Ivan's chest. He slid in deeper, but slowed down, forcing a different kind of groan from my mouth. "Baby, please..." I begged him.

He just shook his head no, sending hair flying into his eyes. I reached up and ran my fingers through it, noting he needed a haircut, but also not wanting to see it go. Then he stopped moving altogether and flipped us over so I was on top.

"I'm just enjoying looking at you. Set whatever pace you want and I'll just watch, okay?" He ran his hands up my thighs, over my hips, dipped into my waist, and then wrapped them around my breasts. He tugged on my nipples, which got my hips moving a bit faster.

I looked down at him and thought, not for the first time, how lucky I felt to be with him. I teased him by calling him a hottie lifeguard, but he totally was one. The long blond hair, the blue eyes, that tan skin, the muscles, the abs, the steady confidence. And the sweet! He was so crazy sweet underneath that gorgeous package. He always said I was the sweet one, but he had me beat, even if his male pride wouldn't let him realize it. I loved everything about him. He turned me on, my body, my mind, and my spirit.

I ran my hands up along my body, following Ivan's path, grabbed both my breasts, and began to play with my own nipples while I lifted my hips up and down on him. I arched my back and let my head drop, giving him the best damn show I could. Then I righted myself and reached forward to grab both his hands in mine, pinning them to the bed so he couldn't touch me. My breasts were bouncing by his face as I set a faster rhythm. Ivan tilted his head to one side and grabbed one in his mouth, sucking hard to keep it where he wanted without the use of his hands.

And that's when I guess he decided he was done just watching and taking things slow. He ripped his hands out of mine, grabbed me by the hips, flipped us back over and drove into me, harder and much faster this time. I reached up, grabbed his face, and brought it down to mine, kissing him as I exploded. He swallowed my cries, then slowed his thrusts as I caught my breath.

"Will you go out to dinner with me Saturday night?" Ivan gritted out, even while he kept pulling out slowly and then pressing back in.

"What?" I asked, still trying to get my breath back. I was finding it incredibly hard to focus. My brain was as limp as my body.

"Go out with me. Saturday," he repeated, the soft smile on his face in contrast to his tightly coiled muscles.

"Of course." I looked at him with questions in my eyes, trying to figure out why he was asking in the middle of sex. I didn't need to be bribed. I'd say yes, no matter what. I was a sure thing.

But it must have been important to him, because he nodded, lost his smile, but gained intensity in his eyes, thrust in deep one more time, then buried his face in my neck. His low moan was muffled by my skin and hair. I ran my hands along his back, feeling his muscles, absorbing his shudders. Knowing I could affect this gorgeous man was just as good as my own orgasm.

Ivan gave me one last kiss, rolled me over so my back was to him. He wrapped an arm around my waist, pulling me in close, and I fell asleep with him playing with my hair.

See?

Sweet.

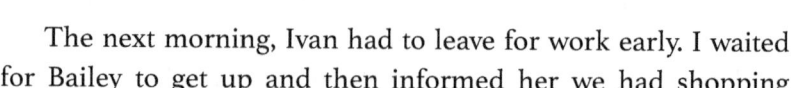

The next morning, Ivan had to leave for work early. I waited for Bailey to get up and then informed her we had shopping to do.

"I got a hot date lined up Saturday night, so I need your help picking out an outfit. And I want to get some sexy lingerie. I don't really have any and I think it's time I'm a grown ass woman and get me some. You up for that?" I asked Bailey over coffee in the kitchen. This was a dumb question as I knew she'd jump at the chance.

"Please, woman. This is what I live for. Let me get dressed and then we're outta here." She ran upstairs and got dressed in record time.

"How come you're not at your shop right now?" Bailey asked as we drove over to Fashion Island.

"It's been brought to my attention I'm a bit of a workaholic," I said with a laugh. "I've placed an ad for more help and I'm trying to set a more reasonable work schedule for myself. In fact, in all the stalker hubbub I forgot to tell you I promoted Jaz to Store Manager. What do you think?"

"I think that makes perfect sense. She'd be a kickass manager for you," Bailey said. Then she paused and shot me a sweet smile. "Look at you, honey. Not even open a year yet and you're hiring managers and more help. You're doing it."

"I know, right? I'm super proud of myself. I'm doing exactly what my mom and I planned out years ago. I'm literally living my dream!" I shook my head at how crazy happy I was. "I was also thinking...I should change my title to something really badass like 'Chocolate Maven' or Mistress of Sweets'. What do you think?" I asked, then started giggling, Bailey joining me.

"Actually, I think that would be perfect. It's your own damn business. Do whatever the hell you want," Bailey said once we'd calmed down.

"Speaking of doing whatever the hell you want...what's up with you and Detective Hottie?" I asked Bailey, a sly grin on my face.

"I don't even know what you're talking about, woman," Bailey responded while shifting around in her seat. She wouldn't look me in the eye, so I knew something was up.

"You think I don't see how you two eye each other every time you're in the same room? You two flirt, but then just dance around each other, never really connecting. What's the hold up there?"

"Look. The guy is HOT. The uniform, the dimple. I admit it. But I'm just not willing to go there yet. Maybe later but it's a no-go right now, okay?" Bailey replied, looking over at me with her eyes begging me to let it go. And I would. For now.

But I made a mental note to investigate and figure out what the deal was, on both sides. My girl deserved to find a good one, and I was ready and willing to be her wing man. Or wing girl. Wing woman, whatever.

20

I van stayed at my house the next few days as we settled
into a normal routine. More of his things started
showing up in my room and in my bathroom. I wasn't so sure
about sharing my precious closet space, but I loved seeing his
clothes in my room, or his shaving cream in my bathroom. I even
pilfered one of his soft t-shirts to sleep in at night, which he
seemed to like once he realized the easy access without the
pajama pants blocking him. I just liked to have his scent around
me, even when he wasn't there.

I was smitten. Hey, if Ivan could say 'tousled', I could use
'smitten'.

On Saturday, I interviewed a couple people for positions at

the shop. I hired two of them on the spot and handed them over to Jaz for training. I got all the details from Mitch's assistant about the company meeting coming up where I'd be catering. Business had already picked up after the Instagram love from Shea Smith and the articles in our local newspaper. Our shop was the new, cool place to get a cup of hot chocolate and then take a selfie in front of our signage. I loved the traffic, but I wanted to make sure we still put out a quality cup of hot chocolate, and didn't make you wait in line forever, either.

Mid-afternoon I left the shop to go home and spend copious amounts of time getting ready for my special date with Ivan that night. I wanted to look good. We'd been through some crazy shit the first few weeks of dating, and now that all of that was behind us, I wanted to focus on us. I had a hot, sexy man to woo. Yes, he was the one to originally chase me, but now that I'd let him in, I figured I needed to step up my game. I believed in equal opportunity wooing.

After a long bath with my latest bath bomb, I washed and blow dried my hair. Painted my nails and toe nails. Shaved seventy-five percent of my body. Applied thirty different make-up products so I would look naturally made-up. Curled my long hair in big, bouncy curls. Lotioned every square inch of skin. Sprayed perfume in all the right places.

And then came the naughty part: the new lingerie Bailey and I had bought earlier this week.

It was all one piece, a lace-trimmed tulle body suit that snapped together in the crotch area. It was cut high on the leg with a waist cut-out on each side and underwire cups to barely harness in the girls. Even though the tulle had a slight fishnet looking design to it, you could still see my skin below, giving more than a little peek of my nipples. I'd never worn anything like it. I may have spent a little too much time doing a dozen poses in the mirror checking myself out. I did manage to refrain from any selfies, however, so there's that.

Next came the new dress Bailey and I found. It was a deep blue color that fell to just above my knee. The top part had two swaths of fabric that came down from my shoulders to meet and tuck into the high-waisted sash, leaving quite a bit of cleavage on display. And my favorite part? The slightly poofy skirt had pockets! I have no idea what I'd even use them for, but man, the thought of the convenience of pockets in my dress was cooler than cool, it was ice cold.

Note to self: I really had to stop listening to hip hop from my high school days.

I slipped on my spiky, silver platform heels and went downstairs. Ivan's truck was just pulling into my driveway so I went to open the front door for him. I was standing in the doorway when he rounded the truck and rushed up to me with a huge bouquet of red roses. He brought me in for a soft kiss and eased me back just enough to look me up and down.

"You look beyond gorgeous, Esa. I'm not sure I even want to go out to dinner anymore. It'll be two hours I can't have my hands all over you," he whispered while running his hand over my waist, my hips, and then my ass. Then he cleared his throat, stepped back, and handed me the roses. "These are for you."

"You sure know how to greet a girl." I was turned on and feeling naughty after being felt up, but my heart was squealing at being presented with red roses from a handsome boy. "And you haven't even seen what's under this dress yet!"

Ivan's head dropped forward, and he released a low groan. Then he took a big breath and lifted his head. "I told myself that I'd spend tonight trying to be the perfect gentleman you deserve. I want tonight to be extra special, so you know how much I appreciate you and what we have together. No ex-boyfriends stalking you, no ex-girlfriends haunting me. Just you and me, Esa."

His eyes were a bright blue and I couldn't seem to look away from them. They held all kinds of emotion; lust, respect, appreciation, kindness, and affection. Here was this wonderful man wanting to make me feel special and be a gentleman. I was just wanting him to ravish me. But I think I liked his plan better. I thought I'd really like to be wine and dined before we made it back to the bedroom. Let the wooing begin!

"I'm one hundred percent up for that," I said with a big smile. Then my smile got sweet and my voice dropped to almost a whisper as I looked up at him through my lashes. "But what you don't understand is that you've always made me feel special and you've always been a perfect gentleman. Not one moment since we've met have you made me feel anything but the center of your attention." I leaned forward and kissed him sweetly, then grabbed his hand to pull him into the house. I had roses from my boyfriend that needed a vase. What I missed was the intense, heated look on his face as he followed me into the house.

Dinner was at Duke's, with a table overlooking the beach and the pier. We were seated just in time to watch the orange ball of sun set into the water. I could see the beach sunset every day for the rest of my life and it would never get old, never lose its reverence.

Duke's was the kind of place you went to celebrate something so it didn't surprise me when Ivan ordered champagne and calamari to start off the meal. The Hawaiian decor reminded me of an older, dark wood paneled restaurant that said class, but also made you feel comfortable. Plus, they had warm, fluffy sourdough dinner rolls. You can always tell an excellent restaurant from a mediocre one by their dinner rolls. Hey, I was in the food industry; I knew these things.

When our glasses were filled, Ivan lifted his glass, indicating he was going to make a toast. For a girl who sells hot chocolate for a living, you'd think I'd be more romantic, but even my stubbornly practical heart was gushing at the sight of Ivan staring at me with what looked suspiciously like love in his eyes.

I swallowed my nerves, lifted my glass, and smiled at him to begin.

"To the most beautiful girl I've ever had the privilege to know. I was taken by you the moment I touched your foot that day on the beach when you tangled with the jellyfish. What I learned in the days and weeks after was that you were not only gorgeous, but you were strong. You can almost out lift me at the gym, you handled your stalker situation with ease, you left an abusive relationship, and you handled the death of your parents, something no one should have to go through so young."

Without missing a beat, he continued on. "Second, I learned you were smart. You started your own business straight out of college, all on your own, becoming an instant hit. And you know, you had the good sense to go out on a date with me."

We both laughed, and I assumed he was done, but he kept going before I could say anything. "Third, I learned you are sweet. You take good care of your friends and employees, and your laugh makes everyone smile around you. I see your regulars coming into your shop, not just for your fabulous hot chocolate, but just to see *you*. You have a positive energy about you that makes everyone want to be around you. So, here's to you, Esa."

He clinked his glass with mine and we both took a sip. I couldn't turn down the wattage of my smile and I was at a loss for words. What could I possibly say in response to that? Turned out, I didn't need a response since Ivan kept talking after we set our glasses down.

"What I'm trying to say, Esa, is that even though it's only been a few weeks, I can, without a doubt, say...that...I'm in love with you," Ivan admitted while staring intently at me. My mouth dropped open at the sincerity in his voice and his soft face. He really, truly was in love with me and wasn't afraid to say it. God damn, my wooing skills must be top-notch.

Then my eyes filled with tears and I couldn't help but feel the warm, familiar glow take over my body like it always did when he was around. He loved me. Holy shit, I loved him back. How did I go from being scared to go on a date to being in love with him in only a matter of a few weeks? However it happened, it was true. I loved him!

At this point, I realized Ivan was still looking at me waiting for my reaction. His sweet smile was fading away and his skin looked a little pale beneath his tan. My shocked silence was probably sending the wrong signal. I'd better put him out of his misery.

I stood up, abruptly pushed my chair back, and threw my napkin on my plate. I skirted around the table and came right up to him as he leaned back in his chair to look up at me. I swiveled my hips, plopped down on his lap, and threw my arms around his neck.

Looking in his eyes, our foreheads almost touching, I whispered, "I love you too, Ivan." Then I laid a big one on him, not caring who was watching from the tables surrounding us. His hands gripped my waist tight while my hands messed up his nicely styled hair. We came up for air way sooner than either of us wanted, but remembering we were in public, we rested our foreheads on each other and just breathed each other in.

"Christ. I was getting worried there..." Ivan muttered. I giggled and gave him one last kiss before returning to my chair.

Dinner was fabulous; between the food, the conversation, and the constant hand holding, it was a night I would never forget. We ate quickly, skipping the famous Hula Pie dessert, as neither one of us could wait to get back home. I, for one, had special lingerie to show off. And I think Ivan planned for my body to be his dessert for the evening. Less calories, and all that.

When we arrived back at my house, we locked the place up and raced upstairs. At the doors to my bedroom, Ivan pulled me back and told me to close my eyes. I gave him a suspicious look, but closed them anyway. I heard him open the doors and then he was back at my side, tugging me forward. Then he stopped and said, "Open your eyes, baby."

Laid out before me was my own bedroom, but looking like nothing I'd ever seen before. The bed was turned down, rose petals were spread out in a trail, from my feet where I stood, over to the bed. White candles were placed throughout the room, glowing bright, casting a sensual light to the room. With Ivan's planning, Bailey must have been my sexy-time fairy godmother. I turned to Ivan and finally found my voice, "Oh my God, honey, it's perfect."

Ivan pulled me in close and wrapped his arms around me. "Yes, you are," he whispered. "Let me take care of you tonight. Will you let me do that?"

Relinquishing control was not something I was good at before I met Ivan, but now, I didn't hesitate. He'd proven over and over again that he had my best interests at heart. This wasn't a Hollywood movie with some grand gesture to prove his love. He'd proven it daily, by showing me that I came first in his life and that I was precious to him.

And remember, he'd said I was smart. And no smart girl would turn down a night at this man's mercy. I nodded my acceptance and squirmed my way in closer to his body.

Ivan bent down and swept my hair over one shoulder, kissing my neck and shoulder, sending goose bumps up and down my arms. Then he pulled my hair back with both hands and began to kiss my jaw, my eyes, my nose, my chin, and finally my lips, all the while walking me backwards to the edge of the bed. His tongue explored my mouth, making me want him closer, skin to skin, no barriers anywhere between us. While our tongues dueled, Ivan's hands slid down my back to unzip my dress. Then he slid both sides of the dress off my shoulders and let the dress pool at my feet.

A whoosh of cool air brought me back from the kiss as I realized he'd stepped away from me. I looked up to see him with his arms crossed over his chest, his eyes on my body, the lids at half mast, desire clear on his face. My nipples began to harden into points as they felt his stare.

Every cup of hot chocolate I had to sell to buy this lingerie was so worth it.

The seconds ticked by, neither of us moving. Finally, Ivan broke the silence. "I want to take a picture of you right now, in that outfit, with those heels, and your hair over your shoulder, and your lips painted red. But I don't want someone else to see you. Ever. So I just have to take a few moments to commit this to memory. Give me a second."

I figured if he liked it that much, he might like it in motion too. So, I did a pivot and gave him the side view with my hip popped out. And then another slow pivot so he could see the back side. And that's as far as I got before his body was suddenly pressed up against me and his hands were cupping my breasts.

"Jesus, woman," he muttered as he nuzzled my neck. Then he reached down and picked me up, his arm under my knees. He placed me on my back on the bed, trailing a finger down my chest between my breasts, over my stomach, down my hip, along my leg, stopping at my heels. He reached down and undid the tiny buckle on the side and took my shoe off. Then the other side. "Relax, get comfortable," he whispered.

He stood back up at the side of the bed, the candlelight reflecting off the side of his face, casting shadows that made his features harder, sexier. Then he toed off his shoes, unbuttoned his shirt, and tossed it to the floor. His gorgeous muscles were perfectly highlighted with the flicker of the candles. Then he slowly unbuttoned his pants, lowered the zipper, and let them drop. My eyes lowered to his boxers to find him fully erect, straining at the waistband.

"See what you do to me? You haven't even touched me yet. This is just from looking at you," he said in his gravely, bedroom voice. I liked to think that voice was just for me. No one else got to hear that exact tone. That was reserved just for us, just for this room. "Roll over onto your stomach, baby."

I rolled over immediately, knowing I'd like whatever he was up to. This relinquishing control thing was easier than I thought.

Ivan grabbed something off the nightstand and then put one knee onto the mattress next to my thigh. He rubbed his hands together and massaged my legs with long, firm strokes. The scent of coconut filled the room as the oil warmed against my skin.

I couldn't help the moans that escaped my mouth as he continued to rub, knead, and stroke my legs. It felt so damn good. My body was relaxing and my leg muscles were feeling delicious after a hectic week. Then Ivan moved his hands up to my ass which also felt heavenly with a touch of erotic thrown in. That buzz of awareness was kicking in, mixing with the relaxation, leaving me unsure if I wanted the massage to continue or if I needed more. I'd never had someone spend so much time rubbing my glute muscles before, but it was the best thing ever.

Ivan moved back down to rub my thighs and then spread them wide apart. His hands trailed back up the inner part of my legs and just barely skimmed over the body suit in the middle before rubbing my ass again. Then his hands were back around to the body suit, rubbing harder this time. I couldn't help it, my booty lifted up in the air, wanting more pressure. He alternated rubbing my ass cheeks and skimming over the body suit.

My fists were clenching the pillow below my head. I was drenched and ready for him, but he kept toying with me, heightening my desire till I couldn't take it anymore. I was about to flip over and take matters into my own hands when his hands reached my body suit again and popped the snaps, releasing the suit and leaving me exposed to his probing fingers.

I was wrong. *This* was the best thing ever.

One hand drew circles around my clit while his other hand was busy thrusting two fingers inside me. I lifted my hips to give him better access. Tingles traveled up my core and down my legs. Then I felt his warm mouth on my ass cheek, sucking and licking while his hands kept up the rhythm. The pillow muffled my moans as I got closer and closer. I felt the wave about to hit and then it crashed through me right when he bit my cheek with just enough force to cause slight pain. I screamed his name and probably other things I had no awareness of, but he just kept his fingers working me until the last shutter left my body.

Then he flipped me over and I saw a wicked little grin on his face.

He wasn't done. Not anywhere close to being done with me.

He reached down and scrunched my bodysuit up over my hips, over my breasts, and then up and over my head, tossing it onto the floor. Then he leaned over and opened the drawer of my nightstand, looking for a condom. Except that was the wrong nightstand. I was in an orgasm induced fog and only realized what he was doing on a time delay. I gasped and was just reaching my hand out to stop him when he burst out laughing.

Dammit. I wasn't in time.

He reached into the drawer and came back over me with a pink, rubbery bullet-looking device. He held it up and lifted an eyebrow at me in question.

"What?" I asked with mock innocence. "I had a five-year *dating* dry spell, not a five-year orgasm-free dry spell. A girl's gotta do what a girl's gotta do!" I explained, perfectly reasonably, I might add. My face was on fire, but I wouldn't apologize for my adult toy.

"Oh, I have no problem with the vibrator, sweetheart. In fact, I'd love to see it in use. May I?" he asked with an eager smile.

"Um, sure?" I wasn't sure what this was about. When my pink friend came out, it was always just me and him. Now it was a threesome, and I wasn't sure how this all worked.

"You're just full of surprises, aren't you?" Ivan looked quite happy about the turn of events.

He twisted it, turning it on low. Starting at my breasts, he teased my nipples with it, then drew it down my stomach, and from hip to hip. He straddled my hips, planting one hand on the mattress by my head, the other hand controlling my vibrator. His lips found my mouth, distracting me from my embarrassment as his tongue tangled with mine. Then he kissed his way down my jaw, onto my shoulder, my collarbone, and then suctioned onto a nipple. My back arched up, offering my breasts to him for more. I reached up to brush my hands through his hair, giving me something to anchor onto.

I let out a low hiss as he moved the vibrator south, finally circling my clit, right where I wanted it. He kept licking, nibbling, and sucking on my nipples, one then the other, as he worked the vibrator up and around, then even further down south where I'd never used it before. I didn't have time to be embarrassed as the sensations coursing through my body took over my thought process. It was building higher and higher, to the point of pain. I was about to come, harder than I'd ever come before.

"Ivan!" I gasped as the first ripple hit me. Then I was lost, light bursting behind my eyelids, my breath coming in jerky gasps, my back arching further off the bed, my hands gripping his hair, holding his mouth to my breasts. He kept circling the vibrator around my clit, lessening the pressure as the shudders left my body.

My hands fell to my sides on the bed. My eyes finally opened again, and I heaved out a breath as my heart rate began to slow. Tingles continued to course down my arms and legs, my muscles incapable of flexing, even if my life depended on them moving.

Good God. I couldn't take anymore. This was it. I was officially spent.

Ivan climbed off me, placed my toy back in its drawer, walked around to the other nightstand, and got out the condom he'd been looking for in the first place.

I could rotate my head over to him, seriously relieved that I wasn't fully paralyzed. "Ivan? I'm sorry, but you're on your own for this round. I'm tapping out. Calling uncle. I don't think I can even move. Do whatever you want with me, but I'm just gonna have to lay here, okay?" I knew I sounded pathetic, but I was too far gone to care.

Ivan stood up to his full height, looked down at me with a proud smile, and shook his head as he chuckled. "Babe." Which I was guessing was short for, no, he didn't like the option I was giving him.

I was opening my mouth to argue, thinking of telling him it really was okay to just do what he wanted as I didn't have anything left. But then I was struck by the sight of him fully naked, fully erect, standing next to my bed in the candlelight. Time slowed down, and I took a mental picture. And then it hit me.

I was so fucking lucky.

This gorgeous man adored me and I him. He took care of my every need, in bed and out. He was sweet, he was sexy, he was successful, he was considerate. He could cook, for God's sake. He was my perfect. Perfect, just for me.

And that's when my second wind bolstered me up and I knew the night was not over. I was about to show this man what he meant to me. Earlier tonight I told him I loved him, now I would show him.

"Come here," I whispered. I got up on my knees, waiting for him to join me on the bed. He stood by the bed in front of me and I wrapped my arms around his neck, bringing his head down to me. I kissed him with all the love I felt, opening my heart and my body to him, trusting him. Ivan ran his hands down my sides, then reached around to pull my hips into his. He was so hard, pressed up against my belly.

I broke the kiss, pulled back from him to lay back on the bed. Then I dropped my bent knees out to the sides, opening my thighs, exposing myself to him. Completely vulnerable. With all the heat I saw in his eyes and the clench of his jaw as he took in the site of me, I never felt more beautiful.

Ivan climbed over me and settled between my legs. He

reached down and guided himself to my entrance, pushing in only an inch or so. He paused to look at me. "I love you, Esa."

Then he plunged all the way in, earning him a groan I couldn't hold back. It felt so good to have him fill me completely. I wrapped my legs around his waist, my arms around his shoulders, and lifted my hips to meet his thrusts. Ivan had his forearms planted on the bed, surrounding my head. He showered my face and neck with kisses as he kept up his unrelenting pace. Every possible inch of my skin was touching his. If I could have climbed inside his body, I would have, just to get even a fraction of an inch closer.

And then I peaked, without warning or build-up, I was there. I called out Ivan's name and squeezed my legs tighter. He kissed me, swallowing my cries, his body pressing into mine, subduing my tremors. Then his lips moved to my jaw as he surged into me one last time, chanting my name.

We laid there, catching our breaths, not wanting to break the connection, unable to move anyway. I was dozing off when Ivan stirred, pulling me back from my sleep. He pulled out, rolled away, then rolled back to tuck us under the sheets, pulling me into his body. He wrapped his arms and one leg around me, jelly-fish style, and we both fell asleep after a whispered, "I love you".

Ivan succeeded; I felt like the most precious girl in the world.

21

The next day, we slowly woke with the sun, lounging in bed together, enjoying a lazy Sunday morning. No work for Ivan today, so I decided to really enjoy this work-life balance thing and take a day off too. Bailey would be so proud of me. After last night's escapades, I wasn't in a hurry to leave Ivan's side. So, I burrowed in closer to his body, my head resting on his shoulder right where it meets his chest. His hand was around my waist, stroking my hip, causing chills to race up and down my back. Ivan was on his back with his other hand under his head, the sheet barely covering him from the hips down.

We were just waking up, refusing to open our eyes and let the day begin. I think we both just wanted to savor our time together and prolong the moment before the outside world interrupted. The I-can't-get-enough-of-Ivan feeling wasn't dissipating, which was a new feeling for me. I normally enjoyed alone time every day and didn't feel the need to spend every waking moment with someone. Until now. We'd spent all evening together, half the night here in this bed wrapped around each other, and I still didn't want to be apart from him even for a second. Attached at the hip, I believed was the phrase. I was starting to see the appeal.

My finger idly traced his ab muscles, fascinated by his tan skin, his light chest hair, and those lean muscles I loved so much. I got distracted by his happy trail and let my fingers get happy. They followed that trail till I hit the jackpot. Ivan's ab muscles contracted in surprise as I wrapped my hand around his morning erection.

"Morning," I whispered. I dipped my hand lower and then pulled gently up his length, playing with him, exploring him. I loved the feel of his soft skin, covering such hardness. It was a contrast I couldn't get enough of.

"Mmm...good morning, love." Ivan's arm tightened around my waist. He crunched up a bit to kiss me on the top of my hair.

I lifted my head off his chest, propped myself up on an elbow, and then kissed my way across his chest. I said hello to each nipple with a quick kiss before following the route my fingers took earlier. I tossed the sheet down by his knees, giving me a beautiful view of him. When my mouth reached his erection, I licked across the tip, then licked down his shaft, giving my hand some moisture. My hand started pumping up and down the base while my lips closed around the tip adding some suction.

"Baby, I won't last long, you keep doing that," Ivan groaned his warning.

My mouth was too busy to answer, but I increased my speed and used my tongue to swirl around the tip then went back to bobbing up and down. I think he got the message: I wasn't stopping.

He swelled in my mouth, his hands gripping my hair, holding it out of my way. I looked up to see his eyes barely open, focused hotly on my mouth as I took in every inch I could. Then his jaw clenched and his eyes closed. He made a loud grunting noise that turned me on even more. His length jerked in my mouth and began to fill me with hot moisture. I drank him down, working to get every last drop. His body jerked and then his hands stilled my movements on him. I let him out of my mouth with a loud pop, loving how much control I had over him in these moments.

Ivan growled, grabbed me, and flipped us over on the bed, so I was laying on my back.

"You weren't supposed to go that far, woman. Although I must say that's the best wake-up call I've ever had." Ivan ended with a sly smile. He rested his forehead on the pillow next to my head as he tried to catch his breath. I stroked his back and just enjoyed the feeling of his body on mine, without work or stalker stress to weigh me down.

Finally, he lifted up onto one elbow and moved his body off to the side of me. He stroked my hair away from my face, just looking down at me. I could tell by his eyes that his brain was whirling, and he wanted to say something so I just kept quiet and let him do it on his own time.

"I've got a question for you. Don't freak out on me, but I really want to talk about this with you. Okay?" Ivan eventually said.

I rolled my eyes. "That's like the worst way to start a conversation with a girl, but yeah, sure, go ahead. I'll try not to freak out."

He playfully tugged on my hair, then launched into it. "So, I know we haven't been together that long, but based on our conversation last night, I think we're on the same page. Esa, I've spent a lot of years thinking I had to pay back the world, or that I had a debt to repay, and now that feeling's gone. I don't want to waste any more time. You know what I mean? I want to move forward with the things I know will make me happy. And I know for sure you make me happy. We spend every moment possible together, and we support each other with the time we spend at our jobs. And I don't think I've even spent more than a couple nights at my place since we started dating. I don't envision myself choosing to spend time away from you when I could be here, right beside you, exactly as we are right now. I mean, do you? I just see us wanting to spend *more* time together and really integrate our lives now that the stalker situation is over and we can settle into a normal schedule. Right?"

He stopped abruptly, probably because he ran out of air.

At this point my mouth was hanging open, rather unattractively I might add, as I tried to keep up with his verbal diarrhea. I thought I knew where he was going and what he was trying to say, but I wasn't sure which question he wanted me to answer first. I thought I should clarify what I thought he meant before I gave answers to questions he may not have actually meant. Now I was confusing myself!

"Baby, are you asking if we should move in together?" I blurted out.

"Well...yes," Ivan responded, staring intently at me, trying to gauge my reaction.

"Why didn't you just say that?" I laughed. "You only needed like five words or so...not five minutes of dialogue!"

"I'm sorry! But all the blood left my brain five minutes ago when you had me in your mouth. I was doing the best I could with limited brain power!" Ivan justified. He cracked a smile though, so I knew he realized he went a little overboard with his speech.

"It is nice to know I have that effect on you, but to answer your questions...yeah. I'm totally on board. I think we should move in together." I smiled at him, then paused to choose my words carefully. "How would you feel about moving in here with me?"

His face lit up, and I was happy I could bring him joy, simply by saying yes. "I was hoping you'd say that. I know this house is important to you and your parents wanted you to have it. I'd never ask you to leave it. Plus, I know Bailey needs a place to live too, so this house is a better option than my tiny condo."

I let out the breath I'd been holding. "Oh, thank God! I was pretty sure you'd understand. I just can't sell this place, or push Bailey out."

"I got you, baby. Always," Ivan said before kissing me quickly. "Now, come on. Let's shower, get some breakfast, and then we gotta move some of my things over here. Make it official." He climbed out of bed and held his hand out to help me up too. The boy was positively giddy.

We enjoyed a long shower together, where we made use of that perfect, little built-in step again. Previously, I thought it was just for resting my foot on when shaving, but I discovered it was for much more. Thank the universe for large shower enclosures!

Then we got down to business dressed in comfortable clothes, suitable for moving boxes. I wore an old pair of frayed jean shorts, perfectly showing off my tan legs, with a cute racerback tank, so I could also show off my shoulders and biceps that I'd worked so hard to build. Yes, we were moving Ivan in, but that didn't mean I couldn't look good. Bailey would have been so proud. Speaking of Bailey, she was already gone again this morning when we emerged from my bedroom. I was going to have to sit down and talk to that girl. She kept disappearing recently, and I didn't think it was entirely to give Ivan and I some privacy. Something was up...

Ivan made us coffee, and I made my healthy protein pancakes. While we ate, Ivan's phone started chirping as his lifeguard group chat lit up with guys roll calling who would show up for their workout later this afternoon. Apparently, they liked to get together every week or so and do workouts on the sand, and then play some beach volleyball. It was supposed to just be fun, but it ended up becoming competitive, with all that testosterone floating around.

"You should come, babe," Ivan threw out there in-between bites.

"You think so? I don't know. It seems like a guy thing. I'd hate to feel like a third wheel." I liked that he wanted me there, but I didn't want to impose on "guy time" either.

"No way. I want you there. Plus, I can show you off and tell everybody about us moving in together. Say you'll come?" Ivan dropped his fork to grab my hand and plead with his eyes.

Damn him and those eyes. "Okay..." I said, still unsure how this would go. But I was rewarded with a sizzlin' hot kiss and he did the dishes, so who was I to complain?

I left Bailey a message, inviting her to join us if she was available. I was hoping the lure of hot, sweaty men would get her there. I also told her that Ivan would be staying here and that we needed to talk about it, face to face, to make sure she was okay with it all. Given her recent schedule, she was never home anyway, so I didn't think she'd mind, but I still wanted to make sure she was comfortable with the changes.

We were able to move a bunch of Ivan's things over to my house. At least enough he could start living with me immediately and not have to go back to his condo to collect things he would need for the day. He said he'd round up some of his lifeguard buddies to come over and move furniture and the bigger boxes.

Like a typical guy, he didn't have a lot of furnishings in his condo, and even fewer pieces that he cared about keeping. Made it easy to move him, but I also wanted him to feel free to make my house his space too. So I told him once he was fully moved in, we could go shopping and get a new bedspread and new towels, ones we picked out together. He said he appreciated the gesture, but what I had was fine. I was guessing linens was not on top of the priority list for my hottie.

I'd never lived with a man, but I was looking forward to it. Ivan was so easygoing that I didn't envision a bunch of fights over decor or living habits. He was generally neat, he could cook, and he seemed respectful of my space, so why not indulge ourselves in the pleasure of each other's company? Plus, I got him in my bed every night, so if there were any disputes we could end them with make-up sex. This moving in thing was looking brighter and brighter.

After moving his stuff over, we put swimsuits on, along with shorts and t-shirts, and headed back out to the beach. We rode our bikes, soaking up the sun and enjoying living so close to the ocean and all the great weather it provided. When we reached the beach to tie up our bikes, we saw that a bunch of the guys were already there warming up and stretching. We left our shoes in our bike baskets and traipsed across the warm sand to meet up with them. I couldn't help but notice we were back at the stretch of beach where everything started. Where one little jellyfish changed my life.

As soon as the group saw us approaching, they lobbed comments at us, whooping and hollering. Ivan held my hand protectively, but even so I sort of lagged behind, unsure if my presence would be well received.

"The Chocolate Princess is joining us!" This was shouted out by a tall, dark-haired guy with a gorgeous physique.

"Did you bring us any of your nectar, beautiful?" Another lifeguard, a shorter, beefier looking guy with the most amazing green eyes asked me with a big smile on his face.

"Guys. She's here to workout with us, not feed you ugly assholes," Ivan responded on my behalf. His smile told me he was just joking with them. Kind of.

"You know where her shop is, fellas. Better bring your wallet next time, huh?" Bailey interjected as she walked up to the huddle.

Oh, thank God she was here. I needed another female.

The group shifted closer, and I felt eight pairs of hottie life-guard eyes assessing me and then assessing Bailey, who loved the attention. I, on the other hand, still felt a little uneasy even though they all had some semblance of smiles on their faces. I wasn't used to that much attention by a crew of extremely hot guys. Ivan was one thing, a whole pack of them was another.

They all started to whine when they realized I really didn't bring along sustenance for them, and they'd have to pay for that hot chocolate they'd come to love. I couldn't let Ivan and Bailey speak for me, without coming to my own defense, so I said the first thing that came to mind. "I already fed Ivan, I can't feed you all, boys."

As soon as the words left my mouth, I knew I shouldn't have put it that way. I was thinking about the pancakes I'd made us earlier, but without context, my statement definitely came out dirtier than I'd intended.

The boys immediately started hollering again, being the immature boys they were, playfully whacking Ivan on the back, ribbing him about 'gettin' fed' this morning. My face turned bright red. Damn boys, making everything a sexual reference. I was happy to hide my face in Ivan's chest when he wrapped me up in a hug. His body was shaking as he laughed along with their good-natured ribbing. At least he wasn't mad. I hadn't embar-rassed him completely.

"Okay, okay, calm down, guys," he said above all the laughter. The boys finally quieted down and Ivan could continue. "Actu-ally, we have news. Esa and I have officially moved in together."

Ivan got more pats on the back and I was yanked out of his arms by Bailey, who had tears in her eyes along with a big ol' smile. "You know I'm happy for you. I don't mind Ivan living with us at all. You know, I'm proud of you for trusting your gut and giving Ivan a chance. You've really come alive these last few weeks. Congrats, girl, you deserve a great guy like him."

"Thank you, B." We hugged it out, both of us fighting back tears.

Then I narrowed my eyes at her. "You and I need to talk though, missy. You're hiding something from me and I intend to figure out what it is. Got it?" I had on my 'I mean business' face, which I'm sure didn't scare her at all. But we couldn't stand here and cry like babies in front of these hotties, so changing the subject was necessary.

"All right, all right, bossy pants," she agreed with an obvious eye roll.

I was ripped away abruptly and hugged by the big lifeguard that helped me that day on the beach when I thought I was being followed by my stalker. "Congratulations, Esa. I'm happy for you and Ivan," he said before passing me off to another lifeguard.

This one was tall, dark, and crazy gorgeous in an Italian Romeo type way. It was the same lifeguard who was kind to me the other day when I stopped by Headquarters to meet Ivan. His face was completely serious, but he pulled me into a hug, kissed me on the cheek, and whispered, "Congrats, Esa. Ivan's been a different guy since you came along. In a very good way."

I pulled back and smiled at him, thinking that was a really thoughtful compliment. "Thank you. I'm sorry, I don't know your name..."

I felt like I'd met him before. Pretty sure I would have remembered that though, given what his appearance did to my hormones both times I'd seen him.

"I'm Dean." Then he smiled at me and I felt a little dizzy. That smile was potent. Before I had a chance to kick-start my brain again and formulate a sentence, Ivan was back at my side, pulling me into him.

"Are we gonna workout, or are you all just gonna make passes at my girl?" Ivan asked the group. They all groaned and moaned but shuffled away from us to find their own spot in the sand to continue stretching.

Bailey looked around at her options like a kid in a candy store. I wasn't worried about her finding a friend. I was more worried for the lifeguards! They hadn't yet dealt with the whirlwind that was Bailey.

Ivan turned to me and got up close, pulling my hips into his. "I gotta keep my eye on you. These guys are like hawks, on the lookout for a pretty girl to flirt with. Wanna stretch together?"

He changed subjects so fast, I barely had time to defend myself. I put my hand on his arm to stop him. I got up on my toes, right up in his face, looked him in the eye, and said, "I don't need watching, my hottie lifeguard. I'm totally and completely in love with you. They can flirt all they want. Doesn't change the fact that you're it for me."

And that's when his eyes heated and all playfulness left his face. He tackled me down to the sand, rolled on top of me, and kissed me like no one was around. His mouth devoured mine, teasing my lips open so his tongue could tangle with mine. My hand wrapped around to the back of his head to grab ahold of his hair and hold him to me. The cheers and whistles that erupted anew faded into the background.

It was just me and Ivan and our beach.

Keep reading for Love on the Defense!
The Beach Squad grows with book #2...

ABOUT THE AUTHOR

Thank you so much for reading my first novel ever! If you loved it, please support the series by leaving a review on Amazon or Goodreads so other readers can find it and enjoy it too. Reviews help other readers determine if a series is to their liking and they help indie authors sell more books so we can keep writing. If you hated it, please disregard this entire paragraph. :)

If you'd like to know more about me or the other novels that I'm writing, please come stalk find me on Facebook, or my private Reader Group called Marika Ray's of Sunshine, or you can find me in-person, on the beach in Southern California, scoping out the hottie lifeguards. For research purposes only, I assure you.

Keep reading for a sample of the next book in the series or simply go to MarikaRay.com for more information about my other books.

If you want to take your stalking to the next level, here are other places you can find Marika:

Newsletter - http://bit.ly/MarikaRayNews

Amazon - https://www.amazon.com/author/marikaray

Goodreads - https://www.goodreads.com/author/show/16856659.Marika_Ray

Bookbub - https://www.bookbub.com/authors/marika-ray

Instagram - https://www.instagram.com/authormarikaray

ALSO BY MARIKA RAY

Also by Marika Ray

The Marriage Sham
The Widower's Girlfriend-Faking It #1
Home Run Fiancé - Faking It #2
Guarding the Princess - Faking It #3
Lines We Cross - Nickel Bay Brothers #1

LOVE ON THE DEFENSE PREVIEW

he young girl dragged her feet along the sidewalk, heading home from school, backpack loaded down with homework. She was a super active girl most days, darting here, running there, but nothing could make her pick up her pace and reach her destination any earlier than she absolutely had to. Her reluctant pace, along with her drooping shoulders and downcast eyes, were all clear signals that the worst part of her day was about to begin.

Schoolyard bullies were of no consequence; it was the bully at home that made her heart pound in fear. She never quite knew when or how the bully would appear, but appear he would, with no mama at home to deflect his anger. Funny how someone can change so dramatically, crumbling down into a different person when someone dies. This little girl had lost her mama when she was just a baby, but she'd also lost her dad. The man remaining in her house still held the title of father, but he resembled none of the types of dad she'd seen on television.

Grief and anger had led to finding oblivion at the bottom of a Jim Beam bottle for her father. But his love of whiskey for drowning out his sorrow also wiped away his capacity to take care of the little girl. No horsey rides around the living room or cozy bedtime stories about that cute, little dog named Biscuit at night. The most she could hope for was that he'd just leave her alone in his drunken stupor and, at best, left some of their dwindling monies for her to buy food to live off the rest of the week.

On the bad days, she could do no right. He'd yell at her, he'd throw things against the wall and rage all night while she huddled, hungry and alone, in her bed. She'd squeeze her eyes tight and picture what her life would look like once she was old enough to leave this house and leave this man behind. Contrary to what he told her all day, every day, she'd find success, she'd make something of herself. And then she'd know.

She was worth something.
She was lovable.
She was worthy.
Someday.

Present Day - Brinley

The sun was blistering, the lack of a damn breeze making every minute a test against the elements. Sweat trickled down the small of my back, down into my swimsuit bottoms. Sand plastered to every square inch of my sun soaked skin, making me irritable, momentarily making me forget my love of this game. I leaned forward and put my hands behind my back, signaling to my partner, using my fingers, to point out which opponent to serve to. The whistle blew and my body tensed, ready to spring into action.

The volleyball flew over the net with a solid bump, set, spike return to our side of the net. My partner dove to the ground, popping it up. I gave her a nice, high set-up at the net, giving her time to scramble back to her feet and get to the ball for a brutal spike. The opponent dug it out of the ground, back to our side of the net in one hit. I bumped it to my partner, she set it and I smashed it down with all the strength and speed I'd been training my whole life for, relishing the loud smack, knowing they had little chance of getting this one back in the air.

Game point for us. Match won. Only four more match wins needed before we qualified for pro status in the IVP, the most elite beach volleyball league in the U.S. That overwhelming yearning feeling clawed at me, making those wins feel like they were within my grasp. If sheer desire was enough to propel me to pro status, there's no doubt it would happen.

The smattering of applause and cheers from the stragglers surrounding the court was meant to be encouraging to the players, and honestly, I was grateful they were even there, but it was also straight up disheartening. This didn't feel like success. This felt like desperation. Yes, I was at the beach, playing the game I loved out in the warm sun every day. There are worse workplaces, for sure. But I wasn't successful at it yet, and the clock was ticking.

I dreamed of the grandstands filled with fans, stomping their feet and yelling my name. The calm ocean breeze carrying itself across the court as a constant reminder of our paradise location. The DJ pumping out fast beats as the cameras waited to catch an athlete interview between games. I wanted that crazy energy to bounce off the sand and hit me in the chest as I fought for first place on the court. Big wins, big crowds; that was success. And it would be mine, mark my words.

My partner, Autumn, slapped me on the back as we grabbed our gear together on the side of the court.

"Nice work out there, BB. We kicked some ass today!" She was grinning and pumped up with the post-win high. "There's a group of us meeting at Freddie's. Want to join us for a quick beer?"

I glanced up and flashed her a grateful smile. "No, I'm good. Thanks for the invite though. I'm going to take a quick dip in the ocean and then head home. Got some early classes tomorrow." I continued to pack up my bag and then straightened up to head out. "Nice teamwork today, lady. We just gotta stay focused for the next four games, yeah?"

"You know it! Don't stress, Brin, we got this," she assured me. She smiled, patted me on the shoulder and turned to leave.

I watched her go, wondering if her commitment was high enough for what I hoped for. I knew I was a bit intense, and that I was laser focused on getting into the pros. But this was a two-man sport. I needed her to be equally as committed in order for this to work. We'd been over this so many times, I didn't want to bring it up again. She already knew I wouldn't be happy with anything less than a pro spot this season.

At this point, there wasn't anything else I could do. I needed to stay focused, put in the work, and hope I'd made a good choice earlier this season when I paired up with her. We got along well and she tolerated my near obsession with my volleyball standings. And she was a good player too, well-suited for rounding out my weaknesses.

As she left with a group of fellow players, I felt a pang of jealousy that she got along so well with everyone else. She had easy friendships while I struggled to chill out enough to remember to be friendly. I should have taken her up on the happy hour offer. That would have helped ease my way into the group dynamic. But it was true, I had classes to teach early the next morning, and I needed plenty of sleep tonight to recover from the game. No injuries, baby.

I turned toward the ocean and took a deep breath, trying to release all the tension I was carrying from the game as I gazed at the sun lowering in the sky. The evenings weren't my favorite time of day. I loved the hues of color as the sun set over the ocean, but evenings always made me uneasy. Something about the impending darkness made my stomach drop. I'd never liked the dark. Nothing good ever happens in the dark.

"Come on, Brinley, keep it together," I mumbled to myself as I dropped my bag in the sand and walked toward the surf.

Not many people were left on the beach as it wasn't quite summertime and it was a Thursday night. Mostly locals and a few random people on vacation. That meant I had a nice patch of surf to myself, the almost private space enabling me to relax.

I walked into the water, loving the shock of the cold water running over my feet, up my legs. I kept going until I was knee deep, bouncing over each wave as they rolled in. Between waves, when the water was still, I bent my knees and dipped down till my shoulders hid under the surface. Delicious goose bumps broke out over my skin as the cold water cooled me down and washed away the aches and pains left over from the game. I kept my eyes trained on the next wave to crash, making sure I was high up enough to jump over them. The wave jumping and the constant backtracking when the undertow tried to pull me out further kept me warm on the inside, even though the water was still a chilly sixty-two degrees.

Once I felt myself going from delightfully cool to painfully numb, I walked back up the sand to my bag. Using my beach towel, I dried off, finishing by tying my towel around my waist. I reached up under my towel and took my swim bottoms off, stuffing them into the netted compartment on the side of my bag. I yanked a pair of cutoff jean shorts up my damp legs and buttoned them, all while staying covered under the towel. My public changing tricks came from watching the surfers back when I was in high school and would escape to the beach every day before school started. Years of practice left me proficient and in no danger of flashing innocent beachgoers.

I whipped my towel off and went to stuff it back in my bag

when I noticed a tall lifeguard standing on top of his tower just up the sand from where I stood. He was far enough away I couldn't see his exact features, but close enough I could tell he was gorgeous. His upper body was on full display without a shirt on, and holy ab muscles, was that a nice sight! Muscles for days, abs chiseled into his front, and then the formfitting red trunks that set off his bronzed skin perfectly. His black hair was cut short and I could have sworn he was looking right at me. His gaze never shifted, so if he was looking at me, he was definitely staring.

I felt my cheeks heating, along with a zing of awareness that shot down through my body. My mouth watered as if preparing itself to make a meal of this man. My mind played out exactly what parts of him I wanted my mouth on first. Time seemed to stand still as I stared back at him, envisioning how his skin would feel as my fingertips ran down his torso, exploring those hard pecs and cut abs.

A kid shrieking further down the beach snapped me out of my daydream. I reined in my wayward mind and shook my head to clear the sexual fog I was lost in for a moment. I peeled my eyes away from his body leaning against the tower, making a mental note to file away that picture somewhere in my brain for later when I could pull it back out, relax and enjoy it without the danger of doing anything about it.

Focus, Brinley! I chided myself. I needed to get home, take a shower, make dinner, and then get to bed. No time for making puppy eyes at the hot lifeguard. I stiffened my spine, flicked my long, golden brown hair behind my back and stood to my full height of just under six feet. Back to all business, I marched off the beach, right to my beat up old Honda and headed home.

Brinley

When I reached my tiny apartment north of the beach in an older residential area, I tossed my bag down on the tiled floor of the kitchen before heading to the bathroom to shower.

As the water heated, I stripped out of my shorts and swim top, rinsing the top in the sink and hanging it to dry. Then I hopped in the shower and let the hot water send all the sand from every crevice of my body down the drain. I lathered my hair and body with soap, getting all the sunblock and sweat off. All my tired muscles and sore joints seemed to relax and turn to jelly.

My eyes were drifting shut as I moaned from the sheer pleasure of relaxing and allowing my thoughts to drift. I saw the lifeguard in my mind, retracing the lines of his body from memory. My hands traveled down my body, rinsing off all the soap, pausing on my breasts, wondering how it would feel for his rough hands to be cupping me instead.

My hands traveled lower as I pictured his hips pressing into me, that hard body up against mine, a close-up of every lean muscle a visual feast for my eyes only. I imagined him pushing me up against the shower wall, spreading my legs and lifting me up. I'd wrap my legs around his waist as he filled me, pumping in and out. Water splashing rhythmically as he attacked me with his hips.

I groaned out loud as the orgasm ripped through me, my eyes widening as I realized how far I'd gone with my little daydream. I blinked my thoughts back to the present while I allowed myself to continue enjoying the tiny aftershocks. That was a first for me. Usually I funneled any sexual tension into my volleyball training by pushing harder, not by indulging in a self-induced orgasm in my damn shower.

When the water turned cold, I turned the shower off, grabbed my towel and stepped out, only to see my reflection in the mirror, cheeks flushed and eyes more relaxed than I'd ever seen them. Holy shit, that guy hadn't even said a word to me and he still gave me an orgasm. That's impressive.

Then I frowned. Not impressive. Dangerous.

Distracting. Definitely not something I could have in my life right now, not even in my imagination. All my thoughts needed to be focused on achieving my dream. Everything else was secondary and needed to wait.

I continued to pep-talk myself as I dressed and got my dinner going. Left over chicken breast, a sweet potato in the microwave, and broccoli boiling on the stovetop. While everything cooked, I cleaned out my bag, putting my towel into the wash so the sand wouldn't spread like an itchy virus throughout my apartment. Sand was like men...always messy and before you knew it, it was everywhere, chafing you in all the wrong places. I snorted to myself at my comparison.

As I sat to eat my perfectly portioned out meal, my phone dinged, alerting me to a text message. It was from my friend, Esa, who I met through Strike Ready, where I taught self-defense classes. She had come in a few months back with Bailey, both of them looking to beef up their skills since Esa was plagued with a stalker. The stalker was recently caught after Esa defended herself when he attacked her. I was a proud teacher, and a much relieved friend.

I groaned in embarrassment as I remembered the first day we met. I was so nervous faced with Esa and her beautiful friend Bailey that I blurted out the most ridiculous joke. I did that some-times when I was nervous in social situations. Which was, like, every social situation. I didn't have a lot of friends growing up, so connecting with others wasn't my strong suit. Thankfully, they'd looked beyond my awkwardness and we'd become friends, meeting up to go for runs on the beach or at Esa's hot chocolate shop at Pacific City. I'd only had her hot chocolate once, and it was divine. Way too much sugar for my strict diet, but I wasn't opposed to meeting up there just to have some company.

Esa: *Party at my place next Saturday to celebrate Ivan and me moving in together!! You better be there & represent #BeachSquad!*

My leg bounced up and down as I read her text. Oh, great. A big party. Where I'd be expected to be social and chitchat with perfect strangers. And I bet I couldn't eat or drink anything they'd have there, not with just four tournaments standing between me and that pro title.

But Esa was my friend, and I didn't have many, so I needed to go. I was grateful for the invite, given that I made little to no effort to nurture my few friendships. In fact, though the invite struck terror in my scared heart, it also stoked a warm flame. The flame that warmed me up on lonely nights when the darkness seemed to close in. I was making friends, people who genuinely loved me for me.

It was decided. I'd go, I'd bring them a bottle of wine or something and stay for a bit. I could do this. I could do anything I set my mind to.

Me: *Hell yes, I'll be there! Gotta go dust off my joke book...*

She'd love that. But I wasn't actually kidding. I needed those jokes to loosen up and converse. Where normal people talked about the weather or something, I had to break out the kid jokes like a total spaz and make everyone uncomfortable. Which then made me comfortable. Backward, I know, but that about summed up my social situation: awkward and backward.

I cleaned up my plate, turned off all the lights and climbed into bed, wide awake, listening to the deafening silence. When I'd first moved out on my own, the silence was music to my ears. No violent father disturbing the peace, no dorm room parties all night. But for the last few years, the silence had turned into a giant vacuum of raging nothingness, sucking out all the joy from the room, forcing me to face the fact that I was alone.

I wasn't alone by choice anymore. I was alone, unwillingly, because of my inability to open up and let people in.

So I laid there, mentally organizing my best jokes for next Saturday like a total nerd, and then without warning, my thoughts turned back to the lifeguard who captured my attention without a single word or gesture. I drifted off to sleep, those lustful thoughts fading into dreams that made me feel warmer than I'd felt today on the hot court in the sand.

Download Love on the Defense Now!!